GREASER

SOULLESS KINGS MC

ANDI RHODES

BLUE JOURNEY PUBLISHING

Copyright © 2021 by Andi Rhodes

All rights reserved.

No part of this book may be reproduced in any form or by any electronic or mechanical means, including information storage and retrieval systems, without written permission from the author, except for the use of brief quotations in a book review.

Cover Artwork - © Amanda Walker PA & Design Services

For you, the reader.

ALSO BY ANDI RHODES

Broken Rebel Brotherhood

Broken Souls

Broken Innocence

Broken Boundaries

Broken Rebel Brotherhood: Complete Series Box set

Broken Rebel Brotherhood: Next Generation

Broken Hearts

Broken Wings

Broken Mind

Bastards and Badges

Stark Revenge

Slade's Fall

Jett's Guard

Soulless Kings MC

Fender

Joker

Piston

Greaser

Riker

Trainwreck

Squirrel

Gibson

Satan's Legacy MC

Snow's Angel

Toga's Demons

Magic's Torment

PROLOGUE

This isn't funny.

Trinity

Twelve years ago...

"Shut up, Trin. You're gonna wake them up."

I shove the flashlight under my chin and laugh at my brother. Tyler can be such a baby sometimes. Our parents swear we're twins, but I'm not convinced. We're *nothing* alike. The only thing we both enjoy is doing exactly what our parents tell us not to do.

"They're snoring, stupid. We could scream and they still wouldn't wake up." I roll my eyes at him and sigh dramatically. "Are we going or are you too chicken?"

Tyler crawls to the zippered door of the tent and opens it. He leans through to peer into the darkness, his head turning in both directions. When he sits back on his heels, I scoot closer to him.

"Was he out there?"

Tyler's head swivels and he stares at me. "Who?"

"The boogeyman."

My brother punches my arm. "Stop being a brat."

"Don't call me a brat, brat," I demand as I punch him back.

We sit there, glaring at each other. This is always what happens when we fight. He calls me a name, I call him one back, and we glare. He tries to out-stare me, but he sucks at it, and I always win. Always.

He blinks and throws his hands in the air.

"Brat," he mumbles under his breath as he waddles out of the tent.

I follow him, barely able to contain my excitement. We've been in these woods for two days and this is the first night we've both been able to stay awake long enough to go exploring after our parents fell asleep. The campfire has died down, so I have to rely on my flashlight to see where I'm going.

"Wait up," I whisper harshly. Tyle is already past the boundaries our parents instructed us to stay in. "Tyler!"

I use the solar lights to guide me and focus on the dirt path that weaves through the entire campground. When Tyler and I used rocks and sticks to map out our route, we agreed to stay on this path until we got past the bathrooms. That way, if either of us have to go, we can before it's too late.

The rickety wooden structure looms before me and I can't see Tyler. I twist the end of my flashlight, and when it doesn't turn on, I bang it against my palm and try to ignore the fear twisting my stomach into knots. Light flickers before staying steady and I quickly shine it in front of me.

"Tyler! Where are you?" I call out, careful not to be too loud. I don't want any other campers waking up and telling on us.

The door to the boys side of the bathroom flies open and Tyler steps out, wiping his hands on his shorts. I'm so startled that I drop my flashlight, and when it hits the ground, he lifts his head and sees me.

"What?" he asks.

I launch myself at him, arms flailing, and we fall to the ground. We wrestle in the dirt until we wear ourselves out. As I lie on my back, I stare at the sky through the trees. Tyler is next to me, doing the same thing.

"Oh, man." I point up. "Did you see that?"

"See what?"

"The shooting star," I tell him. "The first one this summer."

Tyler sits up and squints at the sky. "There wasn't a shooting star. You're a liar," he accuses.

"Maybe if you didn't leave your glasses in the tent, you'd have seen it."

"Whatever," he huffs as he gets to his feet. He looks down at me and grins. "Are you coming or do you wanna sit here looking at the stars like some stupid girl?"

I get to my feet, wipe the dirt off my jean shorts, and stomp past Tyler. I don't bother seeing if he's coming because I don't care. If he wants to be a jerk, he can do that all by himself. I want to explore, and I don't need him to do it.

The sound of snapping twigs stops me in my tracks. I swing the flashlight back and forth to find the source but see nothing. A hand lands on my shoulder and I whirl around.

Tyler doubles over laughing and when his laughter subsides, he wipes his eyes.

"You shoulda seen your face. You were so scared."

"I'm not scared," I argue. "You just…" I stomp my foot. "You're stupid."

I turn away from him, and he grabs my arm to stop me from walking away.

"I'm sorry, Trin," he says as he lets me go and shoves his hands into his pockets. "I won't do it again."

I narrow my eyes at him, trying to hang onto my anger. It's never easy when he says he's sorry. Tyler is a pain in the butt, and he can be mean, but he *is* my brother. My *twin* brother. I don't know what I'd do without him.

And I'll eat bugs before I'd ever tell him that.

"C'mon, Trin," he urges. "Don't stay mad. I really am sorry."

"How sorry are you?" I ask, recognizing an opportunity to work this in my favor.

He pouts but finally says the words I want to hear. "I'll do your chores for a week."

"And?"

He sighs. "And I'll give you half of my allowance."

I pretend to think about it before nodding my head and sticking my hand out. "Pinky promise?"

He links his pinky with mine. "Pinky promise."

Tyler and I spend the next hour traipsing through the woods and my mind wanders to all the things I'm going to buy with my extra five dollars. I see a lot of candy in my future.

"Trin, wait up!"

I stop and realize that Tyler is no longer walking next to me. I look over my shoulder and see him bent over by a tree.

"What're you doing?"

"My shoe came untied."

I retrace my steps and kneel next to him.

"Over, under, around and through," he mumbles.

I watch as he tries to tie the laces. Tyler spends more time barefoot than anything, so it always takes him forever to tie his shoes. He repeats the rhyme our mom taught him and is still slow.

I set the flashlight on the ground next to me. "Here, let me help."

He swats my hand away. "I've got it."

I stand up and cross my arms. The longer I watch him, the more frustrated I get. Especially because now, I have to pee.

"C'mon, stupid. It's not that hard."

"I'm not stupid," he snaps.

"Fine," I whine. "But hurry up. I gotta pee."

I start bouncing from one foot to the other. My dad calls it the wee-wee dance.

"Go pee if you have to go so bad."

I glance over my shoulder to look for a tree I can pee behind, a place close enough but where he won't see me. I spot the perfect one and start toward it.

"I'll be right back."

"Yeah, yeah."

I step around the trunk and shove my pants down to squat. Relief is instant. As I'm tugging my shorts up, a twig snaps.

"Tyler, don't come around the tree," I demand. "My pants aren't up yet."

I get the denim the rest of the way up and snap the buttons. More twigs snap but Tyler doesn't say anything.

I'm gonna take the rest of his allowance if he tries to scare me again.

I step to the side and see Tyler sitting by the same tree, still trying to tie his shoe.

"Ty—"

My shout is cut off by something wet over my mouth. A strange smell fills my nostrils and a strong-arm wraps around my waist.

Tyler!

As I'm lifted off the ground, I flail against whoever has a hold of me. I thrash and thrash and thrash until my body begins to tire out. I try to keep my eyes open, keep my stare focused on Tyler because when I get free, I need to know how to get back to him.

"Shhh, baby girl. Everything is going to be fine."

The voice in my ear is weird. It reminds me of how my dad disguises his voice when he tells scary stories by the campfire. But this isn't my dad. He wouldn't do this.

My thoughts become jumbled, and my eyes keep drifting closed. I fight it, try to keep them open, but it's becoming impossible.

"Trinity!" Tyler is calling out for me. "Trinity this isn't funny!"

Tyler!

"Trinity!"

The further I'm carried away from the tree, the more distant any sense of normalcy becomes. Tyler's voice fades and my eyes drift closed for the last time.

CHAPTER ONE

Never, ever, fuck with a man and his sense of loyalty.

Greaser

Present day...

"Finish him, Greaser. We're outta time."

Joker's voice comes through the speaker in the Nightmare Room. It took every argument I had to convince him to let me handle Forge on my own. Joker is not one to sit back and watch, but I think he knows how badly I need this.

I pull my leg back and kick Forge in the stomach, enjoying the way he curls in on himself and groans in pain.

"Ya hear that, Forge? Your time is up."

"I…" He rolls toward the wall. "I didn't realize who she wanted it for," he cries.

"Bullshit!" I kneel next to him. "I know you don't really think I'm that stupid. My fucking name was in the box labeled 'Father'."

Forge spits blood from his mouth and twists to look at me. "How was I supposed to know your name is Trent?"

I turn the knife over in my hand, letting the smooth handle and glint of the blade calm me. Maybe 'calm' isn't the right word. Center me, ground me, *fuel* me. That's more accurate.

I grab a hold of Forge's hair and yank his head up off the floor. "You've been forging documents for the Soulless Kings for years. You knew who the fuck Cora was trying to trick."

He tries to pull out of my grasp, but I slam his skull into the concrete floor. He howls in pain.

"Greaser, bro, c'mon."

I swivel my head to glare at the camera in the corner of the ceiling. Joker knows how much this means to me, and I don't want to be rushed.

"G, I get it," Joker says, his voice crackling through the speaker. "Cora did a number on you and Forge made it possible. But if we're not in church when Fender's ready to start, it'll be you in here with Fender dishing out the punishment."

My muscles tense. Joker and I both know that's not true. Fender will be pissed, sure, but he knows exactly who I have down here. This isn't like the time we had Joker's mom down here and we had to hide it. I take out Forge, the club needs to find a replacement. No way could I have kept this from my president.

"Go stall for me," I bark, knowing Joker can hear me. "I'm not even close to done with this prick."

"Joker, please," Forge pleads from his prone position. "You've gotta convince him I didn't know."

"Shut up, Forge," Joker barks. "G, I'll give you two more minutes. Either finish him or I'm coming in there to do it myself."

"Seriously, bro, I didn't—"

I slam my boot into Forge's throat to cut off his words. He kicks his feet and thrashes his body but to no avail. I stare at him as his face pales and his eyes start to glaze over.

When I lift my boot, he gasps for air. I cross to the other side of the Nightmare Room and lean back against the wall, arms crossed over my chest. I watch as Forge scrambles to his knees and reaches to use the wall as support.

"Once you're on your feet, how long do you think you'll stay there?" I ask.

Forge rises to his full height, which is nothing impressive. Although, in fairness to him, I'm six five and any man under six feet seems... small.

"Sixty seconds, G," Joker says.

Forge grunts out a humorless laugh. "I guess I'll stand for at least a minute."

I stalk toward him, knife grasped tight in my fingers. "You think that's funny?"

"No," Forge replies. "I don't. I'm about to die because you couldn't keep your dick in your—"

Before he can finish his sentence, I grip his shoulder and pull him toward me as I thrust the knife into his chest with my other hand. Forge's eyes widen for a split second, and he tries to breathe. Unfortunately, the only noise that comes out of him is a gurgling sound as he's drained of life.

I fling him to the floor, maintaining my hold on the knife so it slides out of his body. I swipe both sides of the blade on my jeans to rid it of blood and shove it back in its sheath. Before I leave the Nightmare Room, I squat next to the dead body and shake my head.

"Never, *ever*, fuck with a man and his sense of loyalty."

I rise to my full height and the door swings open behind me.

"Feel better?" Joker asks from the hallway.

I turn around and stalk from the room.

"Not even a little bit."

I take the stairs two at a time and make my way to the meeting room. I toss my knife in the designated box and take a deep breath before striding to my chair.

"Do we need to find a replacement for Forge?" Fender asks from the head of the table.

"What do you think?" I snap.

"I think you need to remember who the fuck you're talking to."

Footsteps sound behind me and I glance over my shoulder to see Joker shaking his head at Fender. As my best friend, I know Joker is simply trying to help deflect some of Fender's wrath. I appreciate it but I'm a big boy. I can handle myself.

"Sorry, Prez," I say. "Been a long year with all this bullshit hanging over my head. I think I'm just coming down from it all."

Fender heaves a sigh. "Greaser, I get it. You bent over backwards to support Cora and she threw it in your face. But you need to be able to separate personal from the club. Right now, I need your focus to be the club."

I narrow my eyes at him. Fender is oversimplifying a very complicated situation. Cora didn't just throw my support in my face. She showed up on my doorstep with a newborn and showed me a birth certificate listing me as the father. Not only was that a massive ruse to get to my bank account, but the boy wasn't even hers. He was her nephew and Cora was playing house.

"I'm good, Prez," I assure him, knowing that's the furthest thing from the truth.

Fender stares at me a moment longer before nodding at Piston.

"Church is in session." Piston bangs the gavel.

"I want to spend our time today discussing Trainwreck," Fender begins. "He's been prospecting for a while now, and it's time to evaluate whether or not we're going to vote on his membership or end his prospecting."

"There's no denying that Trainwreck is, well, very deserving of his road name." Piston shakes his head and we all chuckle. "He can be an idiot at times, but if I'm being honest, we all have our moments."

"He's loyal as hell," Joker chimes in. "He'll do anything he's told to do."

"True," Piston agrees. "Fuck, I don't know how he managed it, but there is no trace of our transgressions in the woods. He's a damn wizard."

"The Nightmare Room has never been so clean." I shrug. "Probably need to get him down there today."

Joker rolls his eyes. "If we agree to put his patch to a vote, he's not gonna have time to clean tonight. He'll have one last test to get through."

"I guess it's a good thing I used my knife and not my pistol," I quip.

"Huh?"

I shrug. "Less blood to clean up."

Joker throws his head back and laughs. "I hate to break it to you, G, but you didn't leave the knife in the body to plug the hole. There's gonna be a lot of fucking blood."

I wave my hand dismissively. "Fine, I'll get one of the other prospects to clean it up."

"And that is all shit that can wait until after church," Fender barks. "I'd like to get home sooner rather than later."

"Okay," Piston says and glances around the table. "Does anyone here need to talk through Trainwreck's time as a prospect?"

A chorus of 'no's echo around me.

"Then let's vote," Fender commands. "All in favor of putting Trainwreck's patch to a vote, thump twice."

The vote is in Trainwreck's favor.

"Okay, I'll call church for tomorrow at noon. All patched members will be present and will get a vote." Fender swivels to look at the club enforcer. "Riker, can you put him through his last test tonight?"

Riker rubs his hands together like a kid in a candy store. "I think I can handle that." Riker looks around the room. "Anyone want in on the fun?"

"Count me in," Joker says.

"Looking forward to it," Piston laughs.

"Good. Trainwreck will be your responsibility tonight. If anything goes wrong or something happens to change your mind about the patch, let me know by eight in the morning."

"You got it, Prez," Riker agrees.

"If that's all, we're adjourned." Piston bangs the gavel to dismiss us.

I remain in my chair until only Fender and I remain.

"Seriously, G," Fender begins. "You okay?"

"Would you be?" I counter.

Fender tips his head back and blows out a breath. "Probably not."

"Then there's your answer."

"Do you want me to have someone cover your shift at the gate tonight?"

"You don't think I can handle it?" I bark, rising from my chair and leaning on the table.

"Not what I said." Fender walks to the door but pauses before continuing into the hall. "But you've been burning the candle at both ends trying to sort through everything. Figured you could use some rest."

"I'll rest when I'm dead."

Fender nods but it's not in agreement. There's resignation in his eyes, a sadness that only pisses me off.

"That's just it. Keep going the way you have been, and you'll be dead sooner than any of us would like."

CHAPTER TWO

I'm a ghost. A faceless statistic among thousands of others just like me.

Trinity

"Are you sure this is where you want dropped off?"

I ignore the trucker's question and stare out the passenger window of his rig. How do I explain to a complete stranger that I'm not sure of a damn thing other than I need to be exactly where I'm going?

"Here." He thrusts a sandwich at me. "At least take this."

My mouth waters at the sight. I haven't eaten since yesterday, and even then, it was only what I could dig out of a dumpster behind a diner in some nameless town. Scraps. That's what I've been existing on for the last week.

I tentatively reach for the offering, and when my fingers touch the bread, I yank my hand back. Embarrassment washes over me at my action. Jimbo, as he's insisted I call him, has been nothing but kind to me. He picked me up off the side of the interstate this morning, and I think he sensed my fear right away. He talks a lot, mostly about his wife and kids, but there's a soothing quality to his voice, a tone I haven't heard in twelve long years.

"It's just a sandwich, honey." He thrusts it closer. "Please take it."

I lift my eyes to his and the smile on his face reminds me of my dad… my first dad. Tears spill over my lashes, and I swipe them away. I've cried more since my escape than I have in the years since I was taken.

"I hate leaving you here," Jimbo comments when I take the food from him. "Listen, I talked to my wife and—"

"When?" Fear pricks my skin as all the ways Jimbo could be lying to me take hold. "When did you talk to your wife?"

"Back at that last rest stop," he says softly. "You were sleeping, and I didn't have the heart to wake you up. You seemed like you needed the rest."

I stare at him, trying to find the lie spilling from his mouth, but it's not there. There are a lot of things in life that I don't know how to do, but reading people isn't one of them. I had no choice but to learn that particular skill.

"I…" I wring my hands in my lap. "I'm sorry."

"Oh, now, don't do that. You have nothing to be sorry for."

And I have no choice but to take him at his word.

"Okay."

"Anyway, I talked things over with her and we agreed that, if you want, you could come stay with us." He holds his hand up to stop my protest. "Just until you get on your feet. We have a spare room available. We're foster parents and don't have a placement at the moment." He shrugs. "It's yours if you want it."

I swallow past the lump in my throat and avert my gaze. I should say yes, accept his offer of a warm bed and a roof over my head. But I can't. And as good as it all sounds, I don't want to.

I open my mouth to speak several times before words come out. "I appreciate the offer. I really do…"

"But?" he prompts.

I take a deep breath and look out the window at the road I should be walking down instead of sitting here in the warmth of Jimbo's rig.

"I have somewhere to be."

The sound of shifting leather forces my attention back toward him. He's holding his wallet open, and I watch as he pulls a stack of twenties from it.

"If you insist on getting out here, at least take this." He thrusts the money at me the same way he did the sandwich. "This will get you an Uber back into town if you need one and a night or two at the motel."

I stare at it a moment before snatching it from his grasp. Jimbo chuckles and shakes his head before twisting in his seat to face the front of the cab.

"I don't know what it is you've been through, but I hope you know that there are people in the world who you can turn to. And people you can't."

I shove a hand into my pocket and wrap my fingers around the note I wrote on a discarded receipt four days ago. I've spent so much time putting distance between me and… *them*, that it didn't even cross my mind that I could be running straight toward someone I can't trust.

If there's anyone you can turn to, it's him. Even if he gave up on you like the rest of the world.

I take a deep breath and steady myself. If I don't go now, I'll chicken out, so I push open the door. Before I step down, I whirl around and throw my arms around Jimbo.

"Thank you," I mumble in a choked whisper.

I don't give him the chance to hug me back. With the sandwich and cash in my hands, I jump out of the rig and slam the door.

I walk down the road with my head held high. It's several minutes before I hear the truck drive off and only then do I look back. I watch as his taillights disappear. Not for the first time in my twenty-one years, I feel very alone.

I pull my jacket tighter, suddenly chilled, and start walking again. I have no idea if I'm doing the right thing, or if I'll even be recognized, but I have no one else.

I'm a ghost. A faceless statistic among thousands of others just like me.

You're not missing, Trin. You're dead.

A thunderous sound seems to echo in the trees lining the road and the louder it gets, the more I *feel* it. The shaking, the rumble, the tremble in the ground beneath my feet. My slender frame vibrates from it.

I rush into the trees to hide as motorcycles come into view. I'm not ready yet. He can't see me until I'm ready.

I watch as they drive by, squinting in hopes that I'll recognize one of the riders. Disappointment floods my system when none of them look like the photo I managed to track down.

Even if you recognize him, he won't recognize you.

I glance down at myself, and my shoulders slump. No, he won't recognize me. But he should. If anyone should, it's him, it's my twin.

I quickly look up and down the road to make sure I can walk again without being seen. There's no one in sight. I step back out into the fading sunlight and savor the light, even as it dips below the horizon.

I haven't exactly been kept in the dark. I wasn't hidden away in a dungeon or anything. In fact, for the first few years, life was as normal as it could be considering the circumstances. It was the last seven years that were… dark.

When my destination comes into view, my lungs seize.

I'm not ready. I'm not ready. I'm not ready.

Those words play on repeat in my mind. They dig their claws into my brain and squeeze, ripping to shreds any sense of hope I have left. They dig and pull and twist and rip until there's nothing left but determination.

Determination to find him, to be seen.

Determination to be *me* again.

CHAPTER THREE

I hate liars and have no problem making them see the error in their ways.

Greaser

What the fuck is she doing?

I lift my phone to glance at the time and realize forty minutes have passed since I first spotted the crazy chick along the side of the road. I don't know what the hell she's doing or what she's got planned, but as long as she stays away from the gate, we'll have no problems. I don't give a shit what someone does until they step foot on Soulless Kings' property. She hasn't yet.

My phone vibrates in my hand and seeing it's a text from Joker, I swipe my thumb up the screen to open it.

Damn this is fun.

Attached to the text is a picture of Trainwreck sitting in a chair. Two strippers are hanging all over him and a third is pouring liquor into his mouth. This is only the first part of the last test. The entire night centers on setting up the prospect in situations designed to get him to talk.

First, get them hammered and horny at a strip joint. We always pay several girls ahead of time to grill the prospects about club business. If the prospect talks, the night is over and so is his time with the Soulless Kings.

If he doesn't talk, he's transported to a mock Nightmare Room at the back of the property. It's a modified semi-trailer. From the outside, it looks like a piece of junk so if the prospects happen upon it, they think nothing of it. But once they're placed inside, if they make it that far, they get a taste of what our enemies feel once we capture them. It's not pretty, but it weeds out the pussies, those who aren't dedicated to the club and the life. And sometimes, we'll invite a rival club member to help out, which actually serves two purposes: see how the prospect holds up against a rival and as a warning to the rival of what will happen if they cross us.

I send a quick response to Joker, asking him to keep me updated, and he replies with a thumbs up emoji. I set my phone back down, and when I lift my head to see what the chick is doing, I'm shocked to see her walking toward the gate.

Standing from my chair, I step down out of the gate house. I reach back around to press the button that releases the lock.

"What the hell are you doing?" I call to her as I step up to the opened gate.

The woman freezes and her eyes widen. She opens her mouth to speak several times, but nothing comes out. While she's standing still, I let my gaze roam over her. Her hair is dark and lifeless. Her clothes are dirty, and I can't tell if they're baggy because she prefers them that way or if she's just too skinny.

"I... um..." I see her throat work as she swallows. "I'm, uh, looking for someone."

"This isn't the fucking lost and found." I point down the road to indicate the direction she came from. "Police department is that way."

Her head swivels as she glances at the road and then returns her attention to me. She wraps her arms around herself and her tiny body trembles.

"I need to see Tyler," she says, her voice steadier than before. "Just get Tyler."

I take a step toward her, and she stiffens. I ignore the action and continue to advance on her until I can make out her features in the meager light. She looks familiar, but I can't quite put a finger on why.

"Who the fuck is Tyler?" I demand, anger building at the entire situation.

"He's..." She swallows. "My brother. Tyler is my brother."

I roll my eyes. Clearly she's not going to be honest with me. "Look, lady, if there were anyone here by the name of Tyler, I'd know it. Especially if he had a fucking hot sister."

She has no idea how true those words are. She may appear dirty and... lost, but it's impossible to deny that there's a natural beauty beneath the grime. One who would be claimed in a heartbeat if she were cleaned up.

"I know he's here." She shakes her head as if to clear it. "I tracked him to this place."

Immediately, the hairs on the back of my neck stand up. If she's tracking someone here, we've got a problem. I reach out and wrap my fingers around her bicep and jerk her toward me.

"Who the fuck are you and why are you here?" She tries to yank away from me but fails. "And before you try and lie again, keep in mind that I hate liars and have no problem making them see the error in their ways."

She stares at me for several long seconds, her chest heaving, almost as if she ran a marathon rather than tried to free herself from a large man. When she averts her gaze, her shoulders slump and she seems to shrink in on herself.

She mumbles something under her breath, and I lean in close.

"I can't hear you," I snarl.

"Trinity." Her voice is shaky but there's more force in her tone. "My name is Trinity."

"Did Cora send you?"

She shakes her head vigorously. "No one sent me. I'm just looking for my brother."

Without letting go of her, I pull my cell phone out and tap the screen to bring it to life. I find Fender's contact and press the call button.

"Everything okay?" he asks when the call connects.

"Hardly," I scoff. "Some bitch is down here at the gate claiming she's looking for her brother."

"Tyler," she yells. "My brother is Tyler."

"Shut the hell up," I bark.

"Tyler?" Fender asks.

"That's what she says."

"The only Tyler I know is Trainwreck, and he's an only child."

I glance at the woman for a moment and study her features as if that will tell me whether or not she's being honest. I dismiss the possibility almost immediately. Trainwreck hasn't always been the brightest, but there's no way he'd lie about having a sister. What purpose would that serve?

"I'm guessing she's somehow tied to Cora," I say to Fender.

I'm hoping he'll tell me he disagrees. Cora has done enough, taken enough from me, and the thought that she's somehow trying to inflict more pain, more damage, is more than I can handle.

"Maybe," he concedes. "But do you really think Cora is that stupid? We made sure she knows what happened to Forge and we didn't exactly take it easy on her either."

"I don't know, but it's the only thing that makes sense."

"No, it's not," Trinity snaps. "The thing that makes sense is the truth."

"Open your mouth one more time," I seethe with a hint of a dare in the words.

"Take her to the Nightmare Room. We'll hold her there until we can sort this out," Fender instructs. "I'll send one of the prospects down to cover the gate."

"Got it."

I end the call and shove my cell back into my pocket. I drag Trinity toward the shack so I can close the gate and lock up the property. She flinches when the metal clanks into place. Part of me wants to taunt her, tell her that the gate is the least of her worries, but something holds me back.

What if she's telling the truth? What if Trainwreck is the one who needs to answer for lies?

Again, I dismiss the idea entirely. Trainwreck knows what will happen if he's caught in a lie. No one in their right mind would intentionally put themselves in that situation. Especially not for something as stupid as how many siblings they have.

When a man is invited to prospect for the Soulless Kings, he's asked questions about his life, his family, friends, acquaintances. We have to be sure there is nothing in their lives, in their past that will bring trouble to our door. Of course, we verify the information we're given. If Trainwreck said he was an only child, we made sure that was true.

What if our information was wrong?

"What's the Nightmare Room?" Trinity asks quietly.

The rumble of the club's golf cart saves me from answering. I glance over my shoulder and see Royal, another prospect, grinning from ear to ear. He loves gate duty. Says it keeps him 'on the frontline'.

When Royal brings the golf cart to a stop, he hops down and strides around the front toward us.

"Wipe that damn grin off your face," I snap. "It's annoying."

Royal tries to school his features, but he can't. That's part of the reason his membership in the club hasn't moved past prospect since he started a year ago. He always seems too damn happy. There is nothing menacing about him. Don't get me wrong, the motherfucker would just as soon gut you as talk to you, but that's part of the problem. No self-control. If he can't regulate his facial expressions, how can we trust him to exercise control with more important tasks?

"What's going on, G?" he asks when he comes to a stop in front of me.

"Greaser," I push out. "How many times do you need to be told to call me Greaser? You haven't earned the right to call me G."

"Your name is Greaser?" Trinity asks.

I ignore her question. My name is inconsequential to her. What I'm going to do to her is not.

"You're on gate duty the rest of the night," I say to Royal. "Don't fuck it up."

"Are we expecting trouble?"

My eyes dart from Royal to Trinity and back again. "Expect anything."

I urge Trinity toward the golf cart and shove her onto the seat. I reach into the compartment under the bench on the back and pull out a set of cuffs. I snap one loop on her wrist and another on the cart before walking around to sit at the wheel.

"When the brothers get back with Trainwreck, send them to the Nightmare Room. Tell them it's urgent."

Royal nods his understanding and steps into the gate house. I turn the key and take off toward the clubhouse. Even in the cool night breeze, I can feel the heat coming from my passenger. And it's not a good kinda heat. No, it's tension, fear, anger.

Good. She's gonna need all of that where she's going.

CHAPTER FOUR

We have more than blood between us.

Trinity

"Still sticking to your story?"

I pull my knees up to my chest and wrap my arms around them. This room—the Nightmare Room—is cold and creepy. I'm surrounded by concrete and cinder blocks. When that *monster* first threw me in here, I could at least see my surroundings, but as soon as the steel door slammed shut, I was plunged into darkness.

"I'll take that as a yes."

I lean my head back and squint, trying to figure out where the speakers are. I'm alone but when he speaks, it's as if his anger is reaching through the walls and wrapping around me. I don't like it.

How did I manage to go from over a decade of captivity to the kindness of a trucker and back to captivity? How can this be going so wrong?

Captivity. I hate that fucking word.

My mind wanders back to the night I was taken from the woods. I don't remember everything, but I remember enough. I remember exploring with Tyler and someone's arms coming around me. I remember the words they whispered in my ear, the smell of the person's breath, the heat of it on my skin.

A shiver races up my spine as I recall what happened next.

"Well, hello, baby girl."

My face scrunches up in confusion. Where am I? Who is this woman standing in front of me?

"Are you hungry?" she asks with a smile on her face. "I made your favorite... banana pancakes."

"I want my mommy," I mumble as tears fill my eyes.

Her face hardens and it scares me. She steps closer to the bed I'm lying on and I shrink away from her.

"I am your mommy."

I shake my head. My mom is taller, prettier, younger. I don't know who this person is, but it most certainly isn't my mom.

The woman raises her hand, as if to hit me, but a man appears behind her and grabs her wrist before she can make contact.

"Leave her alone, Ma," he says. "They told us she might be confused at first."

"Who told you?" I ask, more confused than ever.

The man steps to the side and smiles, but it doesn't reach his eyes. "The adoption agency. Your parents didn't want you anymore, so we decided to give you a new home."

"Pa," the woman scolds and her tone reminds me of my mom when she's mad at my dad for something.

"Don't 'Pa' me," he snaps, his smile disappearing as quick as it came. "I won't be disrespected in my own house."

"And we agreed I would do the parenting," she counters.

"Stop it!" I shout and scramble backward until I run into a wall. "Stop, stop, stop!"

"Stop what?"

Greaser's voice coming through the speaker pulls me from the memory. I swipe at the wetness on my cheeks and hate that I let what happened get the better of me in front of him. He doesn't give a shit and I'd do well to remember that.

"Answer me," he barks.

My shoulders tense and heat burns through every cell of my body. "Why? Will my answer change anything?" I ask, years of anger and frustration taking over.

"No."

"At least you're honest," I mumble as I rest my head on my forearms.

"Which is more than I can say for you."

I lift my head and glare toward the door. I have no idea if this asshole can see me or not, but I'm past caring. I want to get the hell out of here. I want to go home.

You don't have a home, remember?

"So, if you're Trainwreck's sister, tell me something about him."

I narrow my eyes into the darkness. He's mentioned this Trainwreck a few times, mostly during his earlier phone call, and I have no clue who he's talking about. How am I supposed to tell him something about a person I don't know?

"I don't know who Trainwreck is. I'm here for Tyler," I answer honestly. Not that he'll believe me.

Surprisingly, he doesn't respond, but the lights turn on and the door swings open. I blink several times so my eyes can adjust to the sudden change. He stomps toward me with a cell phone in his hand.

He bends down and shoves the screen in my face. "This is Trainwreck."

I look at the picture, and for the first time since I met this man at the gate, I feel a sense of hope flair.

The picture is of Tyler—Trainwreck—and there are half

naked women hanging on him. The photo is dark, but I can make out his face… my face.

"That's Tyler," I whisper.

He turns the phone to look at the picture and his eyes dart back and forth between it and me. Finally, he sighs.

"You don't see it, do you?" I ask.

"See what?"

"The resemblance." I relax my posture. My muscles ache from tension and I no longer have the strength to remain tied in knots. "I can't believe…" I shake my head and start over. "There is no way you don't see that we're siblings."

"Why not?" He shrugs. "Plenty of people have similar looks and don't have blood in common."

"True," I concede. Lots of people thought I looked like Ma and Pa, but we weren't related at all. "But we have more than blood between us. We're twins, you idiot."

"Bullshit!" he shouts as he rises to his full height.

"Get him here and you'll see."

He runs his fingers through his hair and begins to pace. I watch him go back and forth several times before I stand up as well.

"If this *Trainwreck* is someone you know, call him," I demand. "Call him and let me talk to him. He'll tell you I am who I say I am."

"I can't."

"Why not?"

"Because he's busy."

"Too busy to come see his twin sister?"

He only nods and I heave a sigh.

"Then take me to him."

He stops pacing in front of me and pushes me back against the wall. He braces his hands on either side of my head and leans in close.

"You're pretty ballsy all of a sudden," he snarls.

I try to avert my eyes, but he grips my chin and holds my head in place.

"If you're his sister, how come we didn't know about you?"

The question hurts. It sends an arrow through my heart, piercing yet another hole in the already shredded organ. My eyes burn as tears well up and I try, unsuccessfully, to blink them away.

Images assault my mind. News reports I managed to catch when Ma and Pa permitted me to watch TV flash, one after the other. Phrases like 'Search called off for missing girl' and 'Family has daughter declared dead' stick in my brain, taunting me, terrorizing me.

"Probably…" The words catch, unable to force their way out.

I swallow past the lump in my throat and lock eyes with him.

"Probably because he thinks I'm dead."

CHAPTER FIVE

I will cut a bitch for lying to us and putting a brother through this.

Greaser

"Cat got your tongue?"

I tilt my head back and stare at the ceiling. The Nightmare Room has never felt small to me. Hell, it's *not* small. We made sure of that because sometimes torture and punishment require space. But right this moment, the place that brings a lot of Soulless Kings some fucked up peace feels like it's closing in on me.

I inhale deeply and hold my breath, wishing I had a joint to relax me. Because this bitch is driving me insane. She goes from zero to sixty and back again so fast it's hard to keep up. Just when I think she can't shock me, she does.

"What the hell do you mean he thinks you're dead?" I ask when I drop my gaze to lock eyes with her.

Trinity's eyes well with tears and my rough edges soften. When her bottom lip trembles, I want to reach out and brush my thumb over it and ease her sadness.

Why? She's lying to you. Her sadness is bullshit.

"Let me at the bitch!"

Well, shit.

Trinity's eyes widen and her lips part. I turn toward the doorway just in time to see Trainwreck storm through. The second his eyes land on the woman behind me, he freezes.

I glance from him to her and back again. Several times. Trinity is frozen in place, but Trainwreck no longer is. He strides toward her and shoves her back against the wall, his fingers wrapped around her throat.

I knew she was lying. There's not a chance in hell he'd treat a sister like this.

"Who are you?" Trainwreck demands.

"Tyler, it's me," she squeaks. Her windpipe is being compressed, making it not only hard to breathe but also difficult to speak.

"No, you're not. I don't fucking have a sister."

The tears that Trinity had managed to keep at bay spill over her lashes and run down her cheeks. She's good, I'll give her that. Her heartbreak is palpable and if I didn't know she was lying, I'd actually feel bad for her.

Trainwreck shoves away from her, and she doubles over to rest her hands on her knees, sucking in air and filling her lungs. When she straightens, her eyes follow Trainwreck as he paces the same path I did several minutes ago.

He lunges at her again but stops short of actually touching her. "You look like her, I'll give you that," he says. *Huh?* "I don't know how you did it, or why, but trust me when I say, I'll figure it out. And when I do, the Soulless Kings will burn your goddamn world to the ground."

The words 'you look like her' snagged in my brain. "Trainwreck, look at me," I command.

He slowly turns toward me, and his face is bright red.

He's clenching his fists at his sides and the anger rolling off him is barely controlled.

"You said she looks like her," I remind him. "But before that, you said you don't have a sister. Which is it?"

"I look like her because I am her!" Trinity shouts.

"Shut the fuck up," I snarl. "I wasn't talking to you."

Trainwreck's Adam's apple bobs and he averts his eyes. Trinity moves from behind me to Trainwreck's side and he takes a step away. There's something in his action, in his expression that sets my nerve endings on fire.

Are you fucking kidding me? He's been lying to us?

Trainwreck thrusts a shaky hand through his hair and then curls his fingers around the back of his neck.

"Greaser, I..." He pulls in a deep breath and his cheeks puff up, then he blows it back out. "Yes, I had a sister. But that was—"

"Had?!" Trinity shrieks. "You *had* a fucking sister? I'm right here, stupid!"

Trainwreck's shoulders tense and he fixes his stare on her face. He narrows his eyes at her, as if trying to find something, some detail that will make this make sense.

What the hell is happening?

"I swear to Christ, woman," I seethe, focusing my attention on her. "If you don't close your goddamn mouth, I'll shut you up myself."

Trinity's shoulders slump and her mouth closes, but she doesn't back away from Trainwreck.

"Trainwreck, you've got two minutes to explain yourself."

I cross my arms over my chest to keep from strangling him while I wait for him to speak. He's clearly lied to me, to the club, and that can't be tolerated. But I need answers before I can do anything about it.

When he remains silent, I give him one last chance. "I suggest you start talking. And know this... the words that spill from your lips will determine your fate, so you better make sure they're true. Because if they aren't or if I get even a twinge that you're lying to me, I'll kill you where you stand."

"You can't kill him!" Trinity shouts but I ignore her.

Trainwreck reaches an arm behind his back, and I quickly pull my pistol and shove it under his chin.

"Just grabbing my wallet." His words are rushed but calm. I nod at him to continue but don't move my weapon. He retrieves his wallet and holds it up between our faces. "See?"

I drop my arm but keep the gun in my hand, ready.

Trainwreck opens the leather billfold and removes a picture. He turns it so I can see, and I'm taken aback by the worn photo of two little kids, a boy and a girl. They're sitting on a picnic table in what appears to be a campground. Each of them is holding half eaten chunks of watermelon and they're staring at the camera with grins spread across their faces. They look... happy, normal.

"Why are you showing me that?"

"Because it's the last picture of my sister and me." He huffs out a breath and next to me, Trinity gasps. "Yes, I had a sister." His eyes dart to Trinity and back to me. "Yes, her name was Trinity. I had a twin sister and our parents called us—"

"TNT," Trinity interrupts and both Trainwreck and I swivel our heads to stare at her. "They called us TNT for Trinity and Tyler."

"How the fuck do you know that?" Trainwreck grates out.

"Our parents took us camping and that night we wanted to explore," she says, not even bothering to answer his question. Her lips tilt into a smile and her eyes soften, as if remembering. "We were always getting into trouble and that night was no different, was it?" She doesn't give him a chance to speak. "We waited until they were asleep and then we snuck out of camp." Her smile falls. "You were tying your shoe and I had to pee." Trinity wraps her arms around herself, almost as if that will protect her from the past. "I didn't—"

"Stop!"

Trainwreck whirls toward the wall and thrusts his fist into the concrete. He howls in pain and shakes his hand, but rather than stop, he punches the wall again. Over and over and over until blood begins to trickle toward the floor.

"That's enough," I bark and reach out to wrap my hands around his arms and pull him toward the middle of the room. I spare a quick glance for Trinity and see her hand splayed over her mouth, her eyes wide with shock. "You need to cool down, Trainwreck."

He struggles against me, so I tighten my hold. He may not have the muscle definition that most of the brothers do, but he's getting there. Besides, he's running on adrenaline and emotion and that will beat muscle tone every single time.

"Let me go," he pleads.

"Not gonna happen."

Trainwreck tries to pull and yank his arms free. His rage isn't directed at me, and that's plain to see. If Trinity really is his sister and he thought she was dead, he's got a lot of shit to work through. But first, I need him to calm down so he can try to help me make sense of it.

After several minutes, the fight in him diminishes and he stops straining.

"You good?" I ask.

He nods so I drop his arms and take a step back. When he turns and faces me, the anguish in his eyes cuts through me. I want to be mad at him for lying. I want to rage at him, hurt him, *kill* him for the offense. But I won't, I can't. Not after this. Not after seeing what the memory of his sister is doing to him.

But I will cut a bitch for lying to us and putting him through this.

"Tyler?" Trinity's voice is low, hushed, almost as if she doesn't want to spook him.

I've got news for you, babe. You represent a ghost. That's fucking spooky.

"Tyler, please," she begs. "Just look at me... really look. And you'll see. I'm that girl, your sister."

"My name isn't Tyler," he corrects and drops his eyes to stare at the floor. "It's Trainwreck."

"Fine, Trainwreck," she concedes. "Whatever the hell you go by now, that doesn't change who we are to each other."

Trainwreck slowly lifts his head and locks eyes with her. "Prove it."

Trinity throws her hands up in defeat. "How the hell am I supposed to do that? Neither of you have believed a word I've said so far."

"I don't know," Trainwreck admits. "Tell me something only the two of us would know."

"Like the fact that our parents called us TNT?" She rolls her eyes. "That's not common knowledge, Ty... Trainwreck. What more is there?"

"She has a point," I say.

I immediately want to call the words back. Why the hell am I helping her?

"That nickname was in almost every news story about my sister's disappearance. It became common knowledge within months."

Trinity shakes her head. "There isn't much that wasn't printed in the papers or on TV." She takes several deep breaths and then snaps her fingers. "Wait. I've got it."

She closes the distance between her and Trainwreck and bends to lift her pant leg, revealing an ankle and calf full of scars. I squint as I stare at them, trying to determine what they're from. Trinity then yanks off her shoe and raises her foot so we can see the bottom.

"There." She points to a small scar in the middle of her foot. "That's from the time we saw a magician on TV walk on a board of nails and we wanted to try it for ourselves." She glances at me. "Spoiler alert, we couldn't do it," she says before returning her attention back to Trainwreck. "The first nail I stepped on went straight through my foot. I was crying because it hurt like hell. So what did you do?" She pauses and locks eyes with him. "You stomped on a nail so I wouldn't hurt alone. After a trip to the hospital, they took us straight home and sent us to our room. We were grounded for a week."

"How do you know that?" Trainwreck demands, although his tone isn't as hard.

Trinity stands on both feet and lets her pant leg fall. "Because, stupid, I'm your sister."

Trainwreck shakes his head in disbelief, but I can see his eyes become glassy. "But you..." He swallows. "I... Mom and Dad told me you were dead."

"Did they ever identify a body?" I ask.

Trainwreck rubs the back of his neck and shakes his head. "No, not that I know of."

"Jesus," I mumble.

This is not the way I thought this would play out when I spotted Trinity outside the gate. I'm still not one hundred percent convinced she is who she says she is, but the scales are starting to tip in her favor. At least enough that her claims warrant some looking into.

"I think it's time we take this upstairs," I say. "We need to loop Fender in on the situation and figure out a way to get to the bottom of it once and for all."

"So you finally believe me?" Trinity asks, a tinge of hope in her voice.

"I didn't say that. I don't know what the fuck to believe at this point." I shrug. "But I'm not convinced the Nightmare Room is going to be the place where a light shines on the truth."

"Okay," she says, her shoulders slumping.

"Greaser?"

I glance at Trainwreck. "What?"

"I know my lie needs to be punished and I'll take whatever the club thinks is fair, but…"

"But what?"

"Can my fate be put on hold until we know for sure who she is?"

"And why should we do that?"

I ask the question, but I'm not going to recommend any sort of punishment. Like I said, I'm not convinced of anything yet, but if it turns out that Trinity is Trainwreck's twin and he thought she was dead, he's going to need the club at his back. Because that's fucked up no matter how you slice and dice it.

And Trinity is going to need the club too. There's no telling what she's been through. Fuck, she could still have danger riding her heels. And if that's the case, she's likely led them straight to the Soulless Kings' door.

"Because I need to know the truth, one way or another. And I won't get that if I'm dead."

"Why would you be dead?" Trinity asks, incredulous.

Trainwreck quickly glances at her before locking eyes with me. "Please?"

I pretend to think about it and finally nod.

"I'll see what I can do."

"Thanks."

"Don't thank me yet."

I pull my cell phone out of my pocket and shoot off a quick text to Fender, asking him to rendezvous with me in the meeting room. He quickly responds that he's already there with Joker, Riker, and Piston.

"C'mon," I instruct and make my way to the door.

I glance over my shoulder to make sure they're following. I see that they are. Trainwreck is behind Trinity, which impresses me. Even through all this bullshit, he's acting exactly as he should. He's making sure that the potential threat is contained between us.

Annoyance flairs. I should have thought of that. I should have remembered that Trinity is still an unknown… until we can confirm who she really is. I should have, but I didn't.

Why is that?

CHAPTER SIX

Fear, it's powerful, so much more powerful than most people realize.

Trinity

"Here ya go."

My gaze drops to the stack of clothes being thrust in my direction before I lift my head and lock eyes with the woman holding them. My brother and Greaser left me in a bedroom and told me to wait until they got back. Before I could ask where they were going, they disappeared, and the lock clicked into place from the outside.

"Thanks," I mumble as I take the clothes and clutch them to my chest like a lifeline. I don't say it, but I can't wait to get out of the rags I'm wearing. It's the last physical link that remains between me and my past and I want rid of them.

"I'm Riley."

When I don't say anything, Riley sits on the bed and scoots toward the wall as if settling in for a long chat.

"And you are...?" she prods.

Annoyance flairs. I'm not in the mood to talk, especially when it doesn't seem to matter what I say to these people.

"Look," she begins as her gaze travels the length of me. "I don't know where you've been or what's happened to you, but you're safe here."

A snort bubbles up the back of my throat and I can't contain it. "Right."

Riley tilts her head. "You don't think you are?"

"I'm locked in a room in some…" I stutter over my words. "Some house where no one gives a shit about me." My shoulders slump as reality comes crashing down. "Even the one person who should be thrilled to see me, isn't. I'm tired and dirty. I'm starving and sick to my stomach, and—"

"That's a lot," she interrupts. "But in case you haven't noticed, the door isn't locked anymore." She nods toward the wooden barrier. "You can walk out of here any time you want."

I glance over my shoulder and realize she left the door wide open when she came in. I don't know how I missed that.

"As for being dirty, there's a shower across the hall. That's also why I brought you the clothes." She shrugs. "Greaser thought you might like to change."

"Oh."

Riley scoots off the bed and walks to the door. "If you decide to stay, I'll have Margo make you something to eat while you're in the shower." She steps through the doorway and rests her hand on the knob. "If you decide to leave, there's a cell phone in the pocket of those jeans." She points to the pants in my hands. "Greaser put his number in so you'd have it if you need anything."

"I…" I shake my head. "Um, what about Tyler?"

"Tyler?" Riley's eyes narrow in confusion, and she

chuckles when it hits her who I'm talking about. "Oh, you mean Trainwreck?"

I swallow past the lump in my throat and nod.

"What about him?" she asks.

"Did he say anything? About me?"

I hold my breath, needing to know the answer but also dreading it. I tell myself that if he didn't say anything, I'll leave. There would be no point in staying if he doesn't care. But if he did say something? If he does—

Riley smiles. "He said 'Tell her to stay.'"

With that, Riley disappears through the door and pulls it shut behind her. I wait for the lock to click, and when it doesn't, I rush forward and yank it open. I glance both ways down the hall. To my left is the door Greaser and Tyler brought me through from that room in the basement. To my right, I see Riley reach the end of the hallway.

Without turning around, she calls out, "Bathroom is right across the hall. When you're done, come and eat."

I slam the door and press my back to it. How the hell did she know I'd stay?

She's right, so does it matter how she knows?

I look at the clothes still in my hand and take a deep breath. A shower *would* feel really good right about now. I push away from the door to turn around and open it. I peek around the doorframe again and see the hallway is now empty.

I practically lunge toward the bathroom and slam the door shut behind me. I twist the lock and then set the clothes Riley gave me on the vanity. Then and only then do I finally allow myself to relax. A little.

The shower stall taunts me from the corner of the room, and I quickly strip out of my dirty clothes. I fold them and set them on the closed toilet seat, aware of the fact that, even though I have another outfit now, I'll probably have to put my own back on at some point.

I reach to turn the water on in the shower and wait for it to get warm before stepping under the spray. I cup my hands in front of me to catch the water as it falls and grin at how good it feels. The heat, the pressure... it's a million times better than what I'm used to. It's perfect.

I quickly wash my long hair and scrub my body clean. I want more than anything to linger, but I have no clue how long I have before my brother and Greaser come back for me, so I rush through the motions.

When I'm done, I push open the glass door and realize I forgot about a towel. I glance at the ones hanging on a bar on the wall and shrug. Not much to do but use one, even if it does belong to someone else.

I wrap the terry cloth around my body and step onto the bathmat. As I'm drying off my legs, a knock at the door startles me and my muscles coil tight.

"Hurry up in there," a deep voice demands. "I've gotta fucking piss."

"Oh, um, I'll be out in a—"

"Riker, use the other bathroom down the hall."

Riley's voice reaches my ears and my shoulders slump.

"Jesus, can't a guy..."

The man's—Riker—words trail off as his footsteps carry him away from the door. Lighter footsteps come closer.

"Hey, no hurry, okay?" Riley says through the wooden barrier.

"I'll... okay," I reply.

Despite Riley's attempt at reassuring me that I can take my time, I quickly dry the rest of the way off and put on the clothes she gave me. I squeeze my wet hair with the towel to soak up as much moisture as I can and then return the towel to the bar. I glance at myself in the mirror and cringe when I see my reflection. The sweats and T-shirt are tighter than I'd like, but they'll do. The problem is with my face. Dark circles mar the skin beneath my eyes and my cheeks are almost yellow with healing bruises. Maybe I shouldn't have taken a shower. At least the grime hid some of this.

Knowing there's nothing I can do about my looks without makeup, I shrug and lift my discarded outfit. I unlock the bathroom door and step out to cross the hall back into the bedroom. Just as I reach for the doorknob, a voice causes me to freeze.

"I thought I told you to stay put."

I slowly turn toward Greaser and take in his scowl. There's a mixture of frustration and… something else in his eyes, but I don't dare try to figure out what.

"I'm sorry," I say. "Riley…" I lean to the side and look past him, hoping like hell that Riley will pop up to rescue me like she did with Riker. Disappointment floods my system when she doesn't.

"Riley what?" Greaser snaps.

I shake my head to reorient myself to the conversation. "She told me I could take a shower." I pinch the T-shirt and tug it away from my body. "She also gave me some clothes to change into."

Greaser appears to think over my answer and then nods as he reaches his hands out toward me. I flinch away and he drops his arms to his sides. With narrow eyes, he says, "I was just going to take those for you so they could be washed."

"Oh, right." I thrust the ragged duds toward him. "Sorry."

Stop apologizing, Trin! You didn't do anything wrong.

That's so much easier said than done. I never have much control over my reactions to someone. There are times when I can stand up for myself, but there are just as many where the last twelve years get the better of me and I simply react out of instinct. Fear, it's powerful, so much more powerful than most people realize.

"It's fine," Greaser says before turning around and walking away from me. "C'mon," he calls over his shoulder.

I scurry to catch up and fall into step beside him. His strides are long, purposeful. I struggle to keep up, and when we're halfway across the room at the end of the hallway, he stops.

I lift my head and see him staring at me out of the corner of his eye. "What?" I ask, unable to stand the silence.

"You hungry?"

My stomach growls in response. Jimbo had given me food, but I devoured what littler there was hours ago.

"I'll take that as a yes."

Greaser starts walking again, toward the bar on the opposite side of the room, and he leans onto his elbows. I glance around for a familiar face, either my brother or Riley, but see neither.

I take a deep breath and force my feet to move in Greaser's direction. He's talking to an older woman, who's behind the bar pouring liquor into two shot glasses. I watch Greaser interact with the woman and wonder what I have to do to make him that at ease with me. Or at least not as threatening and angry.

When I reach the bar, I climb onto a stool and fold my hands in my lap. Both of them stop mid-conversation and stare at me. I look from one to the other, suddenly uncomfortable.

"What?"

"Nothing," the woman says and shakes her head. "It's just... damn the similarities are jarring."

I narrow my eyes, confused. "Similarities?"

"Margo," Greaser snarls, his shoulders stiffening.

She lifts a dish towel and throws it at him. "Oh, stop," she says. "I don't know shit about what's going on so get over yourself."

She shifts her gaze to me for a moment and shakes her head again before refocusing on Greaser.

"Anyone with eyes in their damn skull can see how much she looks like Trainwreck."

CHAPTER SEVEN

I'm definitely going to answer for this later.

Greaser

*A*nyone with eyes...

I grit my teeth and clench my jaw at Margo's words. I want to be angry with her for daring to make assumptions about Trinity and Trainwreck but even I realize I can't be mad about her figuring out the truth. Besides, if there's anyone I should be pissed at, it's me. I should have picked up on the similarities quicker.

"So..."

I swing my head toward Trinity and narrow my eyes at her, torn between wanting her to continue and needing her to keep her mouth shut. Her hair is wet and hangs over her shoulders, tempting me to tuck it behind her ear, to do something that provides comfort, provides care.

"What?" I demand, frustrated at my desire to do something nice.

Trinity glances over her shoulder toward the door. When

she shifts her focus back to me, her expression is one of uncertainty.

"What's the verdict?" she finally asks.

"The verdict?"

"Yeah, ya know," she clarifies. "What did the boss man say about me?"

I think back over my conversation with Fender, Trainwreck, and the others. It went exactly as I thought it would. None of them are thrilled about Trainwreck's lie, but it's understandable, forgivable even. We decided to put aside the vote about Trainwreck's patch until this situation is sorted out, but that's not being done as a punishment. The decision is more about prioritizing.

"That bad?" Trinity mumbles when I don't respond.

I down the shot Margo poured and then the second because it doesn't appear Trinity is going to be drinking it. Margo lifts the whiskey bottle and pours two more. Then she focuses on Trinity.

"I'm gonna go grab you some food."

Margo disappears into the kitchen, leaving me alone with Trinity. An uncomfortable feeling settles like a lead weight in my gut. I look toward the hallway that leads to the meeting room and wonder where the hell my brothers are.

"Why are you ignoring me?" Trinity snaps, pulling my attention toward her.

"I'm not."

She hops off the stool and takes a step away. I grab her by the arm to stop her and she glares at me.

"Let go," she demands, with more spunk than I've seen from her since leaving her in the bedroom.

"I'll let go when you get back up on the stool."

Trinity's eyes shift from mine to my grip on her arm. She yanks out of my hold and climbs back up onto the stool. She reaches for a shot glass and downs the liquor in one gulp.

Her eyes water, and she coughs at the burn as she slaps the bar top, and I can't stop the laugh that escapes.

She narrows her eyes at me. "You think that's funny?"

I nod. "You reacted exactly like your broth—"

I press my lips together to stop the words spewing from my mouth.

"So you believe me?" Trinity asks.

"It doesn't matter what I believe."

"What the hell is that supposed to mean?"

I heave a sigh. "What I believe is irrelevant. The truth is what matters."

"And the truth is that I'm Trainwreck's sister."

"We'll see," I counter.

"Yeah, we will," she retorts.

Trinity rests her elbow on the bar and her chin in her hand. She doesn't look at me, but I can't stop looking at her. Now that she's clean, it's impossible to miss the fading bruises, the evidence of exhaustion. Regardless of who she is, she's been through some shit, and I find the longer I'm around her, the more I want to know.

Margo walks toward us, a plate of food in her hand.

"Here ya go, hun," Margo says as she slides the plate across the bar to Trinity. "This should fill you up."

Trinity sits up straight, her eyes darting from Margo to the food and back again. "Thank you," she mumbles.

"You're welcome." Margo stares pointedly at me but continues to talk to Trinity. "If this lug gives you any trouble, just holler and I'll come rescue you."

Before I can even respond, Margo disappears again. I resist the urge to demand she come back so I can remind her of her place. Margo is nosey, but she's also someone we can all count on to be there, no matter what.

I glance at Trinity and see her still staring at the food as if it's going to jump off the plate and attack her.

"I thought you were hungry."

"I am," she says.

Trinity takes a deep breath and lifts the sandwich to her mouth. She takes a small bite, and I watch her throat work as she swallows. It takes a few more bites before she really lets loose and eats as if it's been days since her last meal.

After she finishes the sandwich, she wipes her mouth with the back of her hand. When she reaches for the chips, I put a hand out to stop her.

"Whoa," I chuckle. "Slow down. You're gonna make yourself sick if you keep eating that fast."

Trinity's head dips for a moment before she says, "Sorry."

"For what?" I ask, curiosity warring with amusement.

She shakes her head. "I… because… "

"Never mind," I say when she can't form a complete sentence. "Just go a little slower. I'm not particularly fond of cleaning up vomit."

She glares at me for a second and then returns her attention to the remaining food. She eats the chips methodically, as if she has to consciously make an effort not to shovel them in her mouth. While she eats, I walk around the bar and get myself a beer and a glass of water for her. When I set it in front of her, she downs the liquid and holds the cup out for me.

I add water to the cup and make my way around to sit next to her. I wait to speak until she's finished every last scrap of food on her plate.

"When was the last time you ate?"

Trinity shrugs, but before I can press her for more, voices reach me from across the room. I glance over my shoulder and see Fender, Trainwreck, Riker, Joker, and Piston coming from the hall. Trainwreck breaks away from the group and heads out the door. I look at Trinity out of the corner of my eye and realize she saw him leave. The hope in her eyes dims and she turns back around.

My brothers stalk toward us, and I stand from my stool. Fender's eyes sweep over Trinity, and he heaves a sigh when he stops in front of me.

"You must be Trinity," he says to her back. She nods but doesn't face him. "Look at me," he demands, and my muscles tense at his tone.

What the fuck?

I don't know this chick. Hell, I'm not sure I even believe she is who she says she is, which makes the sudden sweep of protectiveness annoying. The urge to knock Fender's teeth down his throat is strong… and dangerous.

"Listen, lady," Joker begins. "You don't know us, but you need to do as you're told if you want to stay out of the Nightmare Room."

I clench my fists and open my mouth to speak, but Trinity beats me to it. She spins around on her stool and hops off to stand in front of them. She lifts her chin defiantly.

"Go ahead," she spits out. "Anything you do to me will feel like a vacation compared to the last twelve years."

Piston takes a threatening step toward her, and I shove my arm into his chest. "Don't," I warn.

My brothers' gazes fix on me. Joker arches a brow and Fender narrows his eyes. I'm definitely going to answer for this later.

Piston pushes my arm away and shifts his attention back to Trinity but says nothing. She juts her chin out and crosses her arms over her chest.

"What?" she snaps.

Piston shakes his head and Fender is the one to answer her.

"Why don't we start over?" Fender pauses and Trinity gives a curt nod. "I'm Fender, president of the Soulless Kings and leader of these idiots." His tone suggests he's trying to lighten the mood, but the look on Trinity's face is a clear indication of his failure to do so. "Anyway, we've talked it over and realize that we need to get to the bottom of this, to figure out who you are. To do that, we need to—"

The clubhouse door bangs against the wall, interrupting Fender and pulling our attention in that direction. Trainwreck is walking toward us with something in his hand. When he's close enough, I can see that it's a pink hairbrush.

Trinity gasps and her hand flies to her mouth. Her eyes are wide with shock and there's a sheen to them.

"Here," Trainwreck thrusts the brush at Fender. "Will this work?"

Fender takes the brush and glances at Riker with his brows raised in question. Riker nods and Fender's expression softens as he looks back at Trainwreck. "And you're sure you want to know the truth? Even if it means that she isn't your sister?"

Trainwreck glances at Trinity and nods. "I'm sure."

"Okay." Fender sighs.

"What's going on?" Trinity finally asks.

"What's going on," Piston begins. "Is you're going to be submitting a DNA sample in the morning so we can figure out for sure if you're Trainwreck's sister."

"I am," she cries.

"And we need to confirm it for sure," Fender says. "If we believed every single thing someone told us, our club would have folded years ago."

"I don't know what that means."

"You'll figure it out," Fender says, then heaves a sigh. "For now, we all need to get some sleep." He turns to me. "She'll stay with you tonight and tomorrow morning, the two of you will go with Riker to his guy."

"Uh, Prez?" Trainwreck interrupts.

"What?"

"I'd like to go."

"That's fine." Fender's gaze shifts from Trainwreck to me. "Any problems with that?"

I shake my head.

"Good." Fender nods. "Now, get the fuck out of here so I can go home to Charlie."

The guys disperse, leaving me alone, once again, with Trinity.

"Now what?" she says when silence surrounds us.

"Now, we head to my place."

CHAPTER EIGHT

This is gonna be a long fucking day.

Trinity

The passenger window is cold on my cheek, but I don't move. I can't. I shift my eyes from the blurry trees we pass to the side mirror of the Jeep. Tyler is behind us, on his motorcycle. It amazes me that he hasn't wrecked that thing. He wasn't the most coordinated child.

People change, Trin. Look at you.

"We should be there in a few minutes."

Greaser's voice is low and oddly soothing. I let it curl around me like a soft blanket. When he first confronted me last night, he was rude, intimidating, but since arriving at his house in the wee hours of the morning, he's been different somehow. He still scares me a bit, but for the most part, he's been… nice.

"I'm sorry there wasn't time for breakfast," he says. "I figured you needed sleep more than food. Besides, Riker told me you shouldn't eat before the sample collection. It can skew the results."

"It's okay," I mumble because it's all I can manage.

I don't think I could eat even if I were starving. My stomach is in knots, and my head is pounding. I know what the DNA test will say. It'll confirm what I already know. I'm Trinity Milford and Tyler, aka Trainwreck, is my twin brother. What it won't tell me… that's more nerve wracking.

No DNA test can tell me what will happen once my identity is confirmed. It won't tell me if my brother and I can have a relationship. It won't tell me if my escape actually worked or if the last week has only been a brief reprieve. It won't tell me how to get my fucking life back, the life I should have had.

My body jostles as Greaser pulls into a parking lot and goes over a speed bump. A large building comes into view, and I sit up straight. We park by another motorcycle which Riker is standing next to. Tyler parks in the same spot as him.

"You ready?" Greaser asks as he shoves his door open.

I nod, unable to form words past the lump in my throat. This is it, the first step to a new life. A better life.

I hope.

My door is yanked open, and I shake my head to clear my wandering thoughts. Riker is standing there, arm outstretched to help me out of the SUV. I let my hand rest in his and get out before pulling away.

"This shouldn't take long," Riker says. "He'll collect a sample from you and compare it to the DNA on the hairbrush. It might take a few days to get the results, but at least then we'll know."

"I already know," I say, annoyance flashing through me. "This isn't for me so let's stop pretending it is."

"Let's just get this over with," Tyler grumbles from a few feet away.

Greaser appears beside me and rests his hand at the small of my back to urge me toward the building. "We're not going to accomplish a damn thing if we stay out here and argue."

I yank away from his touch and stomp toward the glass entrance door. I pull it open and step inside. Cool air greets me, but it does nothing to tame the heat flowing through me.

"Welcome to Inroad Technologies," the woman behind the reception desk says with a smile. "Do you have an appointment?"

"We're here to see David Gorman," Riker says as he steps up beside me.

"I see." She glances at her computer. "Name please?"

Riker flattens his palms on the counter and leans forward. "My name doesn't matter. Get David… please."

"Sir," the woman begins. "We have a strict policy about allowing visitors past this area without an appointment. Now, if you'll kindly provide me with—"

"I suggest you get Mr. Gorman, Miss…" Greaser begins from my right.

"Anderson. Linda Anderson," she says calmly.

Her hand reaches below the counter and Greaser leans across the counter and wraps his fingers around her wrist.

"No need to get security," he barks. "Yet."

A crackling sound reaches my ears a split second before a voice comes from the phone on her desk.

"Linda, send them in."

Greaser smirks at her. "See, he's expecting us."

Linda presses a button on her phone. "Mr. Gorman, are you sure?"

"Let. Them. In."

She presses another button and a door to the right of her desk swings open.

"Mr. Gorman's office is the third door on the left," she says as she points in that direction.

We all walk around the reception desk, down the hallway, and are greeted by a tall man in a suit. He shakes Riker's hand and invites us into his spacious office.

"Damn, man," he says when he sits behind his desk. "How long has it been? Five years, six?"

Riker rubs the back of his neck. "At least," he responds, sounding somewhat uncomfortable.

Mr. Gorman's eyes shift to the rest of us, as if trying to figure us out, before settling on Riker again. "So, you were pretty cryptic on the phone. What exactly is it you need from me?"

"I need a DNA comparison done. Quickly."

Mr. Gorman leans back in his chair and folds his hands in his lap. "You know that's not what we do here."

"I do, but you're the only person I know who *can* get this done, with minimal fuss and on a quick timeline."

"In other words, you know I can keep my mouth shut," Mr. Gorman counters.

Riker thrusts a hand through his hair. "That too."

The man leans forward and rests his elbows on his desk. "Tell ya what... come back to Jacks and Jills for a night and I'll do this for you." Riker opens his mouth to argue, but Mr. Gorman holds his hand up to stop him. "That's my condition, man. Everyone misses you there."

Riker seems to think about it for a minute before agreeing. "Fine. One night," he says. "But I need this test run and the results tomorrow then."

"Done."

Riker walks to the door and pauses to look over his shoulder. His scowl is set in stone. "Do what ya gotta do. I'll wait outside."

And with that, he disappears out of the office. I glance at

Greaser, who looks confused and then to my brother, who's fidgeting with his hands.

"Well," Mr. Gorman starts as he stands. "Come with me."

He leads us out of the office and down the hall to another room. When we step inside, it's as if we're somehow transported to another world. The room is stark white with the only contrast being the stainless-steel countertops and machines filling the space. The room is cold and not just in decor.

"So, who's the lucky person?" Mr. Gorman asks after he pulls what looks like a Q-tip wrapped in plastic from a drawer.

Greaser seems to pull himself from his confusion and steps forward. "She is." He points to me and then thrusts out the bag containing my childhood hairbrush. "We need to know if her DNA matches what you can pull from this."

"Sounds easy enough," Mr. Gorman states, his tone indicating he's not taking this as seriously as he should.

Greaser takes another step forward and wraps his hand around his throat. "If you can't do this, tell me now."

Mr. Gorman smirks. "I can do this," he croaks. "But not if you choke me out."

Greaser shoves away from him and folds his arms over his chest. Everything about him screams pissed off but knowing that his anger isn't directed at me shifts my response to it. Instead of scary, he's... hot.

What the hell?

Mr. Gorman takes a step in my direction and hands me the Q-tip. "Here, scrape this on the inside of your cheek a few times." He then hands me a tube. "Put it in here when you're done."

I do as I'm told. When I'm done, I hand it all back to him.

"I'll have the results tomorrow by noon," he says.

"Good." Greaser grabs my arm. "Call Riker with them."

I'm dragged from the room and down the hall, followed by Tyler. Greaser ignores Miss Anderson when she wishes us a good day, and we continue until we're at the vehicle. Riker is straddling his bike, a cigarette dangling from his lips.

"What the fuck was that all about?" Greaser demands after letting go of me. "Since when do you spend time at Jacks and Jills?"

"I don't," Riker says vehemently. "Not in a long time anyway."

"And it better stay that way," Greaser barks. "You know what goes down there."

"I made a deal, and I'll—"

"Fuck the deal," Greaser seethes. "Nothing good can come of following through."

"I hate to break this up," Tyler interrupts. "But can we get outta here? I've got shit to do."

Sadness settles in my gut. I was hoping we could hang out after this was done.

"Go," Riker says.

Tyler wastes no time firing up his bike and screeching out of the parking lot. When he's gone, Riker looks at me and then at Greaser.

"We can talk about this later," he says. "For now, go get her some clothes that fit."

He revs his engine and takes off after Tyler, leaving Greaser and me standing alone. I glance at him, and his stare remains fixed in the direction they went.

"I don't need clothes," I say, suddenly uncomfortable in his presence.

He shifts his eyes to me and takes in my outfit. It's what I had on when he first saw me. The only difference is, now it's clean.

"Yeah, you do."

He walks around the front of the Jeep and gets in. I hear

the click of the lock disengaging and I climb in the passenger side.

"We'll grab something to eat and then get you everything you need," he says as he turns the key.

When the engine purrs, he turns on the radio and cranks the volume, shutting down any ideas I may have of some conversation. I heave a sigh and rest my cheek against the window.

This is gonna be a long fucking day.

CHAPTER NINE

I know what pain feels like. I know what betrayal and loss and fear feel like.

Greaser

"What can I get ya?"

I glance at Trinity and wait for her to order. The waitress stands next to our table, pen poised above a notepad, and loudly chews gum. Trinity remains silent for so long, I decide to take matters into my own hands.

"I'll have the cheese lover's omelet, two pancakes, a side of bacon and a side of sausage, a glass of orange juice and some coffee." I hand my menu to the waitress. "She'll have scrambled eggs, two pancakes, a side of bacon, and a glass of orange juice."

"You got it."

The bubbly waitress practically bounces away from our table to submit our order to the cook. Trinity rests her hands in her lap and stares out the window. I try to figure out what she's thinking, but it's impossible. Not only because I barely know her but also because her expression is blank.

I lean against the ugly red leather of the booth and rest my arm along the back of it. I want to ask Trinity questions, dig for information, but I'm not sure what questions to ask. There are so many.

"Do you ever look around and feel like your existence doesn't matter? Like you're just an insignificant blip on humanity's radar?"

Trinity faces me and the sadness in her expression lashes at me like a tiger swiping a paw at its prey, leaving long strips of shredded emotion in its wake. How the hell am I supposed to answer that?

"Never mind," she says and shakes her head.

"No. Not never mind."

I lean forward and reach an arm across the table. I don't know why because there's no part of her I can actually touch, not with her hands still in her lap. What I do know is the urge to form a connection with her, to comfort her in any way humanly possible, is strong.

"I..." I take a deep breath and try to figure out how to answer her. "I'm not sure I've felt that *exactly*, but..."

"But what?"

I lock eyes with her. "I know what pain feels like. I know what betrayal and loss and fear feel like. None of that is unique to you."

Trinity flinches as if I slapped her and her face hardens. "Oh, so you've been kidnapped, convinced your family didn't want you anymore, raised to be someone you're not, and—"

She presses her lips together to stop the torrent of words when the waitress returns with our food. When we're alone again, Trinity doesn't continue, but she does dig into her scrambled eggs. I vow to get more information once we're done eating.

I manage to clean my plate—correction, plates—before she even touches her pancakes. I wave the waitress over to refill my coffee while Trinity finishes her meal. When she's done, she stacks all the empty plates at the edge of the table.

She props her elbows on the Formica surface and rests her chin in her palms, her gaze shifting to everyone and everything else in the diner other than me.

"Sorry about earlier," she says, so softly I barely catch it.

"Why?"

Finally, her eyes lock on mine. "Because my problems are exactly that... my problems."

"I hate to break it to you, but the moment you showed up at our gate, your problems became the club's problems."

"I didn't ask for that, for you to get involved." She takes a deep breath and sighs. "I just... I just wanted to find my brother."

"About that," I begin. "How did you know where to find him?"

Trinity shrugs. "It wasn't too hard. Once I escaped, I found a library and just did a search for him online. His address is public record."

A rush of anger hits me like a tidal wave, but I manage to shove it down... sort of. "He had the clubhouse listed as his goddamn address?"

Trinity's eyes widen. "Uh... no."

Her answer sounds more like a question, and I have to remind myself it's not her fault her brother is a dumbass. I clench my fists, itching to give Trainwreck a beatdown for being so stupid, so careless.

"I take it that's not a good thing?"

I give a humorless laugh. "No, it's not fucking good."

"I'm so—"

I bang my fists on the table, garnering curious looks from

the other diners. I glance around at them and force myself to take several deep breaths to calm myself down.

"Don't apologize for his mistake," I growl.

Trinity pulls her bottom lip between her teeth and darts her eyes away from me. The action douses my anger because it's sexy as fuck. I avert my gaze and adjust my hardening cock. Now is not the time and Trinity is not the woman.

"Let's get out of here," I say as I slide from the booth. "We've still got a lot of things to do."

I march to the counter to pay the bill and Trinity is next to me within seconds. I take note of the way she's constantly looking over her shoulder and make a mental note to stay aware of our surroundings. Not that I don't already do that, but with her, the danger that lurks in the shadows likely won't be as readily identifiable.

Once we leave the diner, we head to Portland. There are more options there as far as places to shop, and quite frankly, if I'm going to be in any girly stores, I don't want to be too close to home.

I pull into a parking garage downtown and we make our way to street level. There's a Target not too far from where we parked, and we go there first. Maybe I'll get lucky and she can get everything she needs in one place.

I open the door for her, and she hesitates to enter the store.

"What's the problem?"

"I don't have any money," she says.

Does she really think I don't know that? She had no problem allowing me to pay for her breakfast so why is she digging in her feet now?

"I know. I've got you covered."

Trinity shakes her head. "No."

"No?" I let go of the door and grab her by the wrist to drag her away from the entrance. "Why are you making this harder than it has to be? Most women would be thrilled to get free shit."

She yanks out of my grasp. "I'm not most women!"

"No shit."

Trinity's chest heaves as she struggles to regulate her breathing. The pulse point at her throat throbs, and I want to run my hand over it and calm it down. In order to stop myself from doing that, I shove my hands in my pockets.

"Look, if it makes you feel any better, any money spent on you today isn't coming out of my pocket."

"Then who the hell's pocket is it coming from?" she demands.

"It doesn't matter."

"It does to me. I'm not some charity case. I'm not your—"

"Trainwreck," I interrupt. "It came from Trainwreck."

Trinity's body deflates and her shoulders slump. "Oh."

"And he didn't want you to know so can we please keep this between us?"

"I don't understand. Why does it matter if I know?"

Trying to figure out how to explain it to her, I tip my head back and hate the fact that my view of the sky is marred by trees and buildings. I hate cities.

A small hand rests on my bicep and pulls my attention back to the conversation. I stare at Trinity's fingers and memorize how they look on my skin.

"Please," she says softly. "Why does it matter if I know?"

I take a deep breath and let the words fly. "I think it's his way of making up for letting you get taken all those years ago." Tears well in her eyes as I speak, but I don't let that stop me. "When we were meeting last night, he explained to us what happened that night, how you were taken. He blames himself."

"But..." She drops her arm to her side and shakes her head as if to rattle the information around in her brain to make it make sense. "He was just a little kid. We both were. It isn't his fault."

"I agree. We all agree. But I think it's going to take a while for him to forgive himself."

"It sounds like you all believe I am who I say I am," she states. "If that's the case, why the hell did I have to take a DNA test this morning?"

I wondered when this question would be coming the moment I opened my mouth when I shouldn't have.

"Let's just say, I've been duped in a pretty fucked up way recently." I pause and stare over her head, uncomfortable with the turn in conversation but understanding the necessity of it. "I believed something I should have verified. It ended up costing the club an ally so we're all a little wary."

When she doesn't say anything, I drop my gaze to see her focused on something past me, her face pale. I quickly turn to see what she's looking at but can't identify anything that would elicit that reaction.

"What is it?" I ask, but she remains silent. I grip her chin and force her face toward mine. "Trinity, what's wrong?"

"What?" Her eyes dart away from mine for a split second before she returns them. "Oh, uh… nothing."

"Bullshit."

She wraps her fingers around my wrist and urges my hand away from her. "It's nothing. I just…" She shakes her head. "I thought I saw someone I recognized."

"Who?"

"No one," she snaps and turns on her heel to walk away from me.

I follow after her, looking over my shoulder several times before we enter Target. She doesn't elaborate on who she saw, and I don't ask. But I do pay more attention to who's around us and her reaction to them.

Six hundred dollars later, we leave the store with our

arms full of bags. Once she let herself go, Trinity realized she needed pretty much everything. She tried to go for basic and boring clothes, generic toiletries, but I tried to guide her toward things outside of her comfort zone. I don't know if I did myself any favors when I encouraged lacy panties and thongs, but she seemed happy.

After tucking everything into the trunk of the SUV, I slide into the driver's seat and start the engine. But I don't pull out of the parking space.

"What's wrong?" she asks.

"Who did you see earlier?"

Her shoulders stiffen for a minute and her face pales again. I want to call the words back, but something in me won't allow it. I need to know what threat she felt. I need to know what danger is out there.

"Trinity?"

She throws her head back on the seat and blows out a breath. Her eyes slide closed but a tear leaks from beneath her lashes.

"I thought…"

Her cheeks puff up with air for a moment before she spits the words out.

"My parents. I thought I saw my parents."

CHAPTER TEN

Sarah Lowell. Sarah Lowell. Sarah Lowell.

Trinity

"Would you sit the fuck down?"

I glare at Tyler, who's sitting in a chair at the long conference table. Greaser told me this room is used for something called 'church', and normally I wouldn't be permitted, but they made an exception while we wait for the DNA results.

I haven't been able to stop pacing, and apparently, that's annoying to some. I plop down into the empty seat at the opposite end of the table and huff out a breath.

"Happy?" I snap.

Tyler's head whips in my direction, and he narrows his eyes. "Are you—"

His words are cut off by a phone ringing. Riker lifts his cell off the table and smiles after looking at the screen.

"David, give me some good news," he says when he presses it against his ear. We all watch as his smile falls and he mumbles 'uh huh' several times and nods. "Well, thanks for the info." Riker rolls his eyes. "Yeah, fine, I'll find time and I'll be there."

"What's the verdict?" Greaser asks, impatience in his tone.

"The Nightmare Room is going to have a guest soon," Riker deadpans.

Tyler shoots up from his chair and lunges across the table at me. Everything seems to happen in slow motion. Fender jumps up and reaches for his ankle while Joker latches onto his leg. Greaser manages to grab ahold of Tyler's arm a moment before he makes contact with me.

My limbs shake, but I don't move. I'm too stunned. I know I'm Trinity Milford. I know I'm Tyler's twin. So why would I be sent to the Nightmare Room?

"Let me go," Tyler seethes, straining against the men holding him.

"Not gonna happen," Fender barks. "Either get your emotions in check or you're outta here."

"But you heard him, Prez!" Tyler shouts. "Riker said she's headed for—"

"Not what I said, bro," Riker states. All eyes turn to him for clarification. "The Nightmare Room will be used for David."

"What?" Greaser asks. "Fuck, just tell us what the hell he said."

"Trinity's DNA is a match for the sample from the hairbrush."

My shoulders slump in relief and my eyes lock onto my brother. The fight in him disappears and his eyes well up. He's shaking his head as if he can't believe it and then he fixes his gaze on me.

"Trinity?" he questions. "Trin?"

I swallow past the lump in my throat. I want to speak, to say *something*, but I can't force any words past my lips.

"Jesus," Fender mumbles as he releases my brother. "I don't know what to say."

"If David confirmed Trinity's identity, what did he do wrong?" Greaser asks.

Rather than answer, Riker shifts his attention to me. "Who's Sarah Lowell?"

My stomach churns as my head spins. I can feel my blood sink to my feet, no doubt leaving my face pale. *Sarah Lowell.* That's a name I never thought I'd hear again, one I never *wanted* to hear again.

I rest my palms on the table and stand, my body swaying as I do.

"Trinity?" Greaser rushes to my side and wraps an arm around my waist to hold me up. "Who is she?"

Everything around me fades into a blurry hole that threatens to swallow me. I can hear their voices, their concern. It's muffled, as if I'm underwater.

Sarah Lowell.

I'm falling, tumbling into an abyss. I scream for help, but I keep falling so I don't think anyone can hear me.

Sarah Lowell.

"Trin!"

Tyler?

"Trinity!"

Abruptly, I stop falling, almost as if a parachute cord was pulled. Light filters through the haze and a face looms above me.

"Hey, there you are," Greaser says, his tone gritty.

Heat seeps into my flesh as strong arms tighten around me. I concentrate on the sensation and try to bring my surroundings into focus. I rest my head on Greaser's chest, taking every ounce of the comfort he's offering because I know once I tell him who Sarah Lowell is, any peace I'm feeling will be ripped from me.

Someone clears their throat behind Greaser and he turns, with me in his arms, and I see Fender and the others staring expectantly for me to answer Riker's question.

"I… Sarah…" A shiver races up my spine and not the good kind. "Sarah is me. I am Sarah."

"What?" Greaser snaps and practically drops me to my feet. "What the fuck does that mean?"

I lean against the table for support, and this time, it's my brother who steps up next to me.

"I don't understand," Tyler says, shaking his head. "The DNA confirms you're Trinity."

"Riker," Fender begins. "Tell us exactly what David said."

"He said what I told you, that her DNA…" He nods at me. "It matches what he tested it against on the hairbrush. But apparently, he felt the need to take it a step further."

"Just fucking spit it out, bro," Greaser demands.

"He also ran Trinity's fingerprints into some system he developed for Inroad Technologies and came back with a match to a missing person named Sarah Lowell."

"But…" I rub my forehead. "How the hell did he get my fingerprints?"

"Apparently, he was able to pull them from the tube he had you place the swab in."

"Did you ask him to run fingerprints?" Fender asks.

"Fuck no, I didn't," Riker snaps and turns to Greaser. "You were there. I never once mentioned fingerprints."

"I know," Greaser confirms. "Did he say why he ran them?"

Riker heaves a sigh. "He said he thought he was doing me a solid by trying to gather as much info as possible."

"Some favor," I mumble.

"Trin, why would your fingerprints match someone else?" Tyler asks, clearly confused.

"Because that's who I was for the last twelve years." I sit

down in a chair and drop my head into my hands. "I…" I lift my head and shift my gaze from one man to the next. "I wasn't trying to lie to you. You have to believe me. I just… After I was taken, Ma and Pa changed my identity. In less than twenty-four hours, I became Sarah Lowell. I became their daughter."

"That doesn't make sense. If they kidnapped you, why on Earth would they have your fingerprints done and entered into a system?"

I stare at Greaser as I try to figure out how to answer that question. The explanation is very simple while being extremely complicated.

"Because to them, I was their daughter. They did everything they could to make sure we appeared as normal a family as possible. Including submitting my fingerprints for some program that was supposed to help ensure child safety."

"And you let them?"

The accusatory quality to Tyler's question sparks my temper.

"I was nine!" I shout. "They told me that mom and dad didn't want me anymore. They made me believe they were all I had. What was I supposed to do?"

My brother's face hardens. "I'll fucking kill 'em."

"Yeah, probably," Fender agrees. "But first, we need to figure out what the hell we do now. If David entered her fingerprints into a system, she can be tracked. We don't want that."

My heart stops. "Wait, you think they can track me here?"

"I don't know," Fender answers honestly. "Are they good with technology? Do they have the means to track you, the connections?"

"I… probably." My eyes fill with tears. "They managed to make the world believe I was dead. They were able to give me a new identity that no one questioned for twelve years." A tear slides down my cheek and I swipe at it. "Yeah, I think they have connections."

"That's not gonna happen," Tyler vows as he kneels next to my chair and rests a hand on my arm. "They won't find you here. They won't take you again."

"No fucking way," Greaser agrees.

"Prez, we need a plan... fast." Joker sits down in the chair he occupied earlier. "We need every single voting member in here because I have a feeling things are about to get ugly."

"He's right," Piston says as he also sits.

I look around the room at all the men. Each of them expressed doubt about who I am yet here they are, wanting to protect me, willing to fight for me. The feeling is foreign, and my chest constricts.

Fender pulls his cell phone out of his pocket and his fingers fly over the screen. When he sets the device down, he sits at the head of the table.

"Church starts in ten," he says. "Trainwreck, why don't you take Trinity to one of the rooms and we'll—"

"I'm not leaving," Tyler snaps. "No disrespect, Prez, but she's my sister. I want to be involved in this every step of the way."

Fender stares at him for a moment before nodding. "Fine." He shifts his focus to me. "Trinity, you can't be in here during church. Why don't you go out to the main room and wait for us to finish?"

I shake my head wildly as fear twists my insides. "I can't... what if... I don't—"

"I'll stay with her," Greaser says. "I vote in favor of finding, torturing, and killing these motherfuckers. As long as that's the plan..." He bangs a fist on the table two times.

Fender locks eyes with Greaser for a moment, questions dancing in his eyes, questions he doesn't ask. "Noted. I'll allow your vote. Now get her outta here."

Greaser grips my bicep and urges me to stand. He guides me toward the door, but my brother's voice stops us in our tracks.

"Don't let her out of your sight," he commands, and we both look over our shoulders at him. Tyler drops his chin. "I did that once." He lifts his head and locks eyes with me. "Just… don't take your eyes off of her."

"I won't."

Those two words from Greaser are controlled and full of promise. They curl around me, much like his arms did earlier.

"I promise you, Trainwreck. I've got her."

CHAPTER ELEVEN

As the enforcer, I have to be the hardest version of myself that I can be. But I'm not a bad guy. I have a heart, I have feelings.

Greaser

"How long do these things usually take?"

I tip a beer to my lips and down what remains. After slamming the empty bottle back on the counter, I swivel on the bar stool and look at Trinity. She's staring straight ahead, her gaze focused on the wall behind the bar, but I have a feeling she's not really seeing anything.

"As long as they take," I reply.

She glances at me for a second before dropping her chin. "It's been two hours."

"And it could be two more."

Trinity sips the Coke Margo served her and wrinkles her nose as she swallows. She's been nursing it for the last hour, so I imagine it tastes watered down from the ice melting. When she sets the glass down, she slides it across the bar top.

A commotion at the door pulls my attention away from

the woman next to me, and I swivel to see Charlie, Riley, and Holland stride across the room toward us. Riley sits on the stool on the other side of Trinity and the other two stand behind her.

"I'm glad you stayed," Riley says to Trinity.

Trinity only nods.

"Hey, G, where is everyone?" Charlie asks.

"Church," I reply simply.

"Why the hell are you out here?"

"Because apparently I need a babysitter," Trinity snaps, a hint of annoyance in her tone.

What the fuck?

I glare at her before responding to Fender's ol' lady. "*Because*, we didn't think it would be a good idea to leave Trinity alone, not when her abductors are still out there."

"Jesus," Charlie mumbles. "We're here now. Go to church, do your thing."

"No." I shake my head. "You don't know what to—"

"We can handle it," Riley interrupts. "Hell, I'm a champion boxer and these two…" She tips her head toward Charlie and Holland. "They can hold their own. It's not like anyone would get past the gate anyway."

I glance at Trinity to gauge her reaction. I know the three women can handle this and it's not like I'll be far away. Shit, I'll be just down the hall. And I want to be in church. I need to be there. But there's an equally sized part of me that wants to be exactly where I am. With Trinity, keeping her safe.

"Go, G," Charlie prods. "Seriously, we'll scream if there's trouble."

Her tone is full of sarcasm, as is her expression. Charlie doesn't scream. She's probably the most badass chick I know and can take on whatever or whoever comes at her.

"It's fine," Trinity says, waving her hand as if it doesn't matter.

"Are you sure?"

She nods. I stand and Charlie immediately sits on my vacated stool. I stare at Trinity for a moment, trying to give her a chance to change her mind, but she remains quiet and still.

I turn on my heel and make my way to the meeting room, only looking over my shoulder once when I reach the hallway. The four women are talking, or at least Charlie, Holland, and Riley are trying to engage Trinity in conversation.

I stalk down the hall and when I reach the meeting room, I hear raised voices through the wall. I shove open the door and everyone stops talking to stare at me. Trainwreck jumps up from his seat and glares.

"What?" he demands. "Where's Trin? What happened?"

I hold up a hand to stop his questions and force my expression to relax. "Nothing happened. She's fine, brother. She's with the women."

Questions are hurled at me from several brothers and the thud of a gavel shuts them up.

"Let's get back to church," Piston orders, gavel in his hand. "The sooner we get shit figured out, the sooner we can go about the rest of our day."

"Piston's right," Fender agrees and then locks eyes with me. "Take a seat, G, and we'll catch you up."

I do as I'm told, but it takes a minute for Trainwreck to sit back down. He plops into his chair and if tension could kill, I'd be suffocating from it.

"Trainwreck was filling us in on what happened the night Trinity was taken and all of the events that took place in the years following."

"Got it," I say. "Give me the highlights for now."

Trainwreck clears his throat. "She was taken from the campground. We looked for her for days before heading home. The cops looked as well. Everyone did. The only thing that was ever found was a white cloth that tested positive for chloroform."

"I take it there was no other biological evidence or anything on the cloth."

"None." Trainwreck clenches his fists on the table. "For the first year, I remember there being a lot of news coverage, press conferences, organized searches. It seemed like our lives were consumed with finding Trinity."

"And the years after that?" I ask, somehow knowing I'm not going to like the answer.

Trainwreck shrugs. "Each year there was a little less attention, until it got to the point where there was a token news piece on every yearly anniversary. The last time anything was mentioned was year six. That's when Trinity was declared dead. After that, it was like she was forgotten."

"Were there ever any leads?" Joker asks.

"Not that I know of," Trainwreck states. "My parents never shared anything with me other than she was dead." He huffs out a humorless laugh. "But she wasn't dead." His face contorts with pain, a pain I can only imagine.

"You know that's not your fault, right?" Riker chimes in. He doesn't give Trainwreck a chance to respond. "You were a kid, dude. Of course you were going to believe what they told you."

"We had a funeral for her. There was a casket and everything," Trainwreck says, almost as if he's talking to himself. "I never saw a body, but there was a coffin. Why didn't I push to look in the coffin?"

"Dammit, Trainwreck!" I pound the table. "You were a fucking child. You've gotta stop blaming yourself." Anger rolls off me in waves. "Do you blame her for being taken?"

"Of course not," he snaps. "I'd never bl—"

"Then stop doing it to yourself," I bark. "She's back, alive, and you've got a chance most people don't get."

"I know," he mumbles, his shoulders slumping. Trainwreck drops his chin and swipes at his cheeks. "And I'm so damn grateful for that, but…"

"But what?" Riker prods.

When Trainwreck lifts his head, his eyes are glassy and his cheeks are red. "What did she go through for twelve years? When I think about what Trinity faced at the hands of her—"

"Don't," I bite out and his head whips around to lock eyes with me. "Don't make up scenarios in your head. Don't dwell on the what ifs. We don't know what she went through, but we'll find out." I take a deep breath. "And yeah, it's probably not pretty but you'll be strong when she tells you everything because she's going to need you to be."

"Greaser's right," Fender says from the head of the table. "We don't know all the details yet, and for now, we need to focus on the immediate threat. We can sort out the trauma later, once we know she's out of danger and that it hasn't followed her here."

"Is there anything you think we need to know about the last twelve years that will help with our immediate concerns?" I ask Trainwreck.

He shakes his head for a second but then his eyes widen. "Wait."

He reaches into his pocket and pulls out his cell. He taps the screen a few times and then slides the device across the table toward me. I pick it up and stare at the screen, not sure what I'm looking at.

"What is this?"

"It's blurry, I know, but it's a picture I took when I was eighteen, at my parent's funeral."

"Okay," I say, drawing out the word. I slide the phone to

Riker so he can see it and then he hands it to the next person. "Who's the picture of?"

Trainwreck heaves a sigh. "I thought it was Trinity, which scared the shit out of me because my sister was dead. All through the graveside service, I kept catching glimpses of this girl. She was with an older guy and when I went to confront her after the service, she was gone."

"And you never figured out who it was?" Fender asks.

Trainwreck shakes his head. "I should've said something, *done* something, to stop the service, but I couldn't bring myself to. I'd just lost my parents. I was seeing a dead person, so I chalked it up to grief."

"But you took a picture?"

"Yeah, I... I don't know. I wasn't thinking clearly."

"Of course you weren't," Piston agrees. "No one would be in that situation."

"Anyway, after the service, when I couldn't find the girl, I went home and packed up all my shit. I knew if I stayed there, in the place where I grew up, I'd always be seeing Trinity, whether she was there or not. I didn't want to see her. I wanted to move on."

"Understandable." I lean back in my chair. "Hey, you said you were eighteen when you took that picture. That was three years ago so not long before you ended up here."

Trainwreck nods and sympathy settles in my gut. This kid fled a shit show and landed with the Soulless Kings. Don't get me wrong, the club isn't a shit show, but we do have baggage and this life isn't easy. But I can see how it would be exactly what he needed at the time. Hell, what he still needs.

"Anyway," Trainwreck begins. "Do you think we can do anything with that photo? Clear it up some and try to figure out if that's Trinity and who the guy is?"

"Squirrel?" Fender flicks his gaze to our tech guy. "Can you do that?"

"I can try," Squirrel replies. "But why don't we just ask Trinity to look at the picture and tell us?"

"We will," Fender states. "But just in case she can't, you think you can do this?"

"Sure thing, Prez."

"Good." Fender glances around the room. "We also need to dig up as much info on her alias, Sarah Lowell, as we can. We need to compare timelines for Trinity and Sarah, see if we can figure out where one stops and the other begins."

"I'll work on that," Squirrel says.

Fender nods and shifts his eyes to me. "Greaser, I need you and Trainwreck to get as much info out of Trinity as possible. We can dig all we want, but she's going to be our greatest source of information."

"Agreed."

"We also need to be prepared for anything. If David's database somehow triggered something for the abductors to track her down, they could show up at any time. Trinity is not to be alone… ever."

"Speaking of David," Riker interjects. "What's the plan for him?"

"He crossed a line. That can't go unpunished."

"Nightmare Room?"

"Let's put it to a vote." Fender takes a deep breath. "All those in favor of David meeting his maker in the Nightmare Room, thump twice."

Two thumps all around.

"Good. Riker, get him here." Fender scowls. "And once he's here, he doesn't get to step foot off this property. The only way he leaves is in a body bag."

"I want in on his demise," I snap. "I know he's Riker's contact, but if he put Trinity in danger, I want in."

"Me too," Trainwreck adds.

"I have no problem with that. Anyone have any objections to David's fate being in the hands of Riker, Greaser, and Trainwreck?"

A chorus of 'no's echo through the room.

Fender gives a curt nod. "Good. Now, is there anything else for now, before we call it?"

When no one says anything, Piston bangs the gavel. "Meeting adjourned."

Brothers make their way out of the room, leaving only me and Trainwreck behind. He's wringing his hands and looks like he wants to say something, but he remains quiet.

"Spit it out," I snap.

"I'd like to stay with Trinity," he says. "At your place."

Internally, I groan. I don't want a prospect underfoot at my house, but I remind myself that Trinity is his sister, who he thought was dead, and I give in.

He was also hours away from being a patched member. He's one of us.

"Fine."

"Thanks, man." Trainwreck's body relaxes with relief.

"Don't mention it."

I know I'm seen as ruthless, cold-hearted at times, but that's because I have to be. As the enforcer, I have to be the hardest version of myself that I can be. But I'm not a bad guy. I have a heart, I have feelings. And as much as I don't like people in my space, I won't turn Trainwreck or his sister away.

"C'mon," I say and walk toward the door. "Let's get outta here."

CHAPTER TWELVE

It'd be a battle of who's crazier and the Soulless Kings would lose.

Trinity

"Can I get you anything?"

I look toward the bedroom door and see my brother standing there, his expression guarded. We've been at Greaser's house for a few hours, most of which I've spent right here, curled up in bed, with memories flashing through my mind.

"Trin?" he prods when I don't respond.

Tyler walks toward me and stops when he's a few inches from the bed. He squats so he's eye level with me, but when he reaches a hand out, I shrink away from him. Hurt flashes in his eyes and guilt slams into me.

"Sorry," I mumble and scoot into a sitting position.

"Don't be sorry, Trin."

He rises to his feet and sits next to me on the mattress. His movements are slow, almost as if he's afraid he'll scare me. When I don't move away, his body seems to relax.

"Wanna talk about it?" he asks.

"About what?"

"I don't know." He leans his head against the headboard. "Any of it, I guess."

I shrug.

"Okay." Tyler crosses his ankles. "Can you tell me how you got away? How you ended up here?"

"I'd like to hear that too."

My head whips toward the door and Greaser is leaning against the frame, arms crossed over his chest.

"How long have you been standing there?" I snap, annoyed that I didn't notice him sooner.

"Not long." Greaser shrugs and pushes away from the wall to walk toward us. "I came to check on you and saw you two talking. Figured I'd see what you had to say."

"You were eavesdropping?"

"Call it what you want," Greaser says matter-of-factly.

"Seriously?" I look to Tyler. "You're gonna let him get away with this?"

"Trin, that's not how things work around here. I answer to him, not the other way around."

"But I'm your sister!" I shout, anger flaring through me.

"I know you are. But he's family too." Tyler quickly glances at Greaser before returning his attention back on me. "Anything you tell me, you can tell him. You can trust him."

"You should listen to your brother."

I stare at Greaser with wide eyes. "I should… I don't get it. You went from distrusting me, hating me really, on sight, to all of a sudden giving a shit about what happened to me. Why?"

Greaser opens and closes his mouth several times before he sits on the edge of the bed. "Because you're family."

"And that's enough?" I demand.

"Yes."

I bend my knees and wrap my arms around them, as if that will somehow center me, ground me in the here and now. I know I should be grateful that he cares, happy that the real me is being seen and heard again. But ever since hearing the name Sarah Lowell, any positivity I was feeling has been diminished, tainted by the endless possibilities of what that stupid search in a database will cost me.

"At least tell us how you escaped," Tyler pleads.

I swallow past the lump in my throat, realizing I probably should. They're still out there and any information I provide can only serve to help them better protect me. Right?

"It was a little over a week ago… a Sunday." I close my eyes and let the images in. "Ma and Pa dropped me off at the motel on their way to church." I feel Tyler stiffen beside me, but I force myself to ignore it. He's going to react to everything I say, and I can't let that stop me from spitting this out. "It was no different than every other Sunday. I went to the same room, looked at the same walls, sat on the same bed. And I waited." I pause and allow myself to look at Tyler and Greaser. The questions in their eyes don't surprise me. "I know what you're thinking. Why didn't I try to escape before last week if I was left alone?"

Tyler quickly shakes his head, but the action doesn't match his expression.

"It's okay," I tell them. "I get it. That would have been the smart thing to do. And trust me, I tried. But you have to understand Ma and Pa. They had people everywhere. I was always being watched, even if I was alone. And the man at the front desk was on their payroll. I found that out the first time I was taken there. I tried to run as soon as they pulled out of the parking lot, but my freedom was fleeting, and my punishment was worse than I could imagine."

"So what was different about this particular Sunday?" Greaser asks, his voice full of grit and… hate.

"I'm getting there." I take a deep breath before continuing. "I waited for an hour, which was too long. Normally, the client would arrive within fifteen minutes of me being dropped off. I realized that was my chance, one I might never get again. And I'd learned from previous attempts not to walk out the door and think I'd get away." I shake my head. "I broke the window out in the bathroom and climbed through. I didn't stick around to see them realize I was gone. I knew if I did that, they'd find me."

"And you came here," Tyler says.

I chuckle, knowing there's more to my story but recognizing that my brother might not be ready to hear it quite yet. "Yeah, something like that."

"You know you're safe here, right?"

"Sure. But for how long?"

"No one will get to you," Greaser snaps.

I heave a sigh. "I know you believe that, and I want to believe it, but you just don't know what they're capable of."

"And you're underestimating the power of the Soulless Kings."

"Maybe. Hopefully."

Silence fills the room. I could go on and on about what they don't know about the people who took me, who made me one of their own for years, but to what end? The only way to truly understand Ma and Pa is to be forced to go up against them in what would surely be an unfair fight. They're dangerous. More so because they don't look the part. You could meet them on the street and be charmed by them, convinced they're normal, or worse, that they're good.

I have no doubt my brother and his new family could take Ma and Pa on in a physical fight. They'd win for sure. But the fight wouldn't even get to that point. It'd be a battle of who's crazier and the Soulless Kings would lose.

A yawn crawls up the back of my throat and I try to stop

it, but I fail. I'm exhausted, tired all the way to my soul. I don't know if sleep will help but sitting here thinking about the last twelve years won't.

"Why don't you get some sleep?" Greaser says as he stands. He claps Tyler on the back. "C'mon, bro. We can all talk more tomorrow."

My brother looks at me expectantly, almost as if he's waiting for me to ask him to stay, but I don't. He leans forward and kisses my cheek before standing with Greaser. They both walk to the door and stop.

"Night, Trin," Tyler says. "I love you."

Tears clog my throat, but I manage to respond, barely. "Love you too."

Tyler disappears down the hall and Greaser remains with his eyes locked on mine.

"Get some sleep."

He flips the light switch and throws me into darkness.

Light filters through the blinds, bathing the room in shadows. I've tossed and turned all night, only catching brief moments of sleep at a time. Staring at the ceiling, I debate on whether or not to get out of bed. I want to because staying under the covers only makes me feel like I'm giving more power to the fear than it deserves.

I throw the blanket off me and swing my legs over the edge of the mattress. I sit there for a minute, taking in the sounds of the morning. This has been my least favorite part of the day for years because I knew it meant I was still alive, still in hell.

It's different now.

I tiptoe to the door and press my ear against the wood. I don't hear anyone in the hall, so I cross to the bathroom to shower. I'm quick about it and when I'm dressed, I head to the kitchen.

Greaser is standing at the counter, pouring coffee into a mug, and Tyler is sitting at the table, looking at something on a laptop.

"Morning," Greaser says without turning around. He reaches into a cabinet and pulls out another mug. "How do you like your coffee?"

"I'm gonna guess she likes a lot of sugar and creamer," my brother remarks, grinning at me. "She always loved anything sweet."

Sadness washes over me. I'm not the same Trinity he knew as a child. Not really.

"Sugar and creamer with a dash of cof—"

"Just black is fine," I say, internally wincing at the way Tyler's face falls.

"Black," Greaser says. "Right. You got it."

I sit down next to Tyler. "What are you looking at?"

He slams the laptop closed and clears his throat. "Nothing."

Greaser sets a steaming mug in front of me, and I lift it to my lips to blow on it. He sits at the table, across from me, and his eyes dart back and forth between me and Tyler, as if assessing us.

"Trainwreck, show her the picture," Greaser instructs.

I glance at Tyler. "What picture?"

Tyler slowly opens the laptop and, after tapping a few keys, turns it toward me. "This picture."

The second my eyes land on the image, I know what I'm looking at. It's a picture of me and Pa at my parent's funeral. Tears threaten to spill over my lashes, and I don't even try to stop them. What's the point?

"That's you, isn't it?" Greaser asks.

Words refuse to form and all I manage is a nod.

"Holy shit," Tyler mumbles. "I didn't think… I thought… holy fuck."

"You thought I was dead," I say when he can't seem to voice his thoughts.

"Yeah."

I reach out and take his hand in mine. "It's okay, Tyler."

"Trai—" He slams his mouth shut and shakes his head. "Sorry, habit."

"You know you can be both, right?"

Tyler's head whips around and he stares, wide-eyed, at Greaser.

"What?" Greaser shrugs. "You don't think we all struggle with that? With how we remain loyal and true to who we are within the club, while always remembering who we started out as?"

"I guess I never thought about it."

Questions burn in my mind, but I don't know if I should ask them, if I have the right to ask them. Before I can give myself permission to ask, Greaser speaks.

"I'm Greaser, sure, but I'm also Trent. And if I'm being honest, I wouldn't be one without the other."

"Kinda like I'm Trinity but also Sarah," I say.

"No," Greaser replies with force. "That's not even remotely the same. You were forced to be both. For me, it's a choice, one I make again and again, day after day. You didn't choose to be Sarah."

"Didn't I?"

I can't help but doubt what he's saying. I believed what Ma and Pa told me. Wasn't that a choice? I didn't escape sooner. Wasn't that a choice? I lived as Sarah for twelve years. Wasn't that a choice?

"Fuck that!" Tyler shouts as he shoots to his feet. "You didn't choose to be taken. You didn't choose to be a prisoner. You didn't—"

A knock on the door stops his tirade. The pounding gets louder as Greaser goes to see who it is.

"C'mon, Greaser, open up."

Tyler and I make our way to the living room, and a man I recognize brushes past Greaser when the door is open.

"Royal, what the fuck?" Greaser narrows his eyes at him. "I don't recall inviting you in."

Royal bends and rests his hands on his knees, his breathing labored, as if he ran here. "I know. It's just..." He stands and glances at me quickly before refocusing on Greaser. "We've got a problem."

"Spit it out," Greaser demands.

"Fender's trying to get them to leave, but the cop's being a dick and he says he has a court order."

"What the hell are you talking about?"

"Her."

Royal points to me and my legs threaten to give out.

"What about her?" Tyler steps closer to me and wraps an arm around my shoulders.

Royal looks at me and his eyes convey something... an apology? Why?

"They're here for her."

"Jesus, who's here for her?"

"I'm sorry Trainwreck," Royal mumbles.

"What the fuck for?!" Tyler shouts.

I concentrate on my brother's touch, on his body holding me up, because I know what's coming... my worst nightmare.

"Bill and Eileen Lowell. They're here to get their daughter."

CHAPTER THIRTEEN

Completely fucking helpless.

Greaser

"You can't let them take her."

Trainwreck's plea barely registers. Rage burns in my veins, so hot I feel like I'm about to combust. The sun beats down on my face, intensifying the heat to an almost unbearable degree.

I wrap my fingers around the chain-link of the gate and scowl at the couple in front of me. I'm dimly aware of Trinity standing behind me, next to her twin and my brothers. I can practically feel the fear emanating from her, as if we're connected somehow.

"Sarah," the woman says and steps to the side to see beyond me. "Please, honey, we just want what's best for you."

"Her name is Trinity."

"Sir, I'm going to need you to open the gate."

I glance at the cop and tighten my grip. "Not gonna fucking happen."

He presses a piece of paper to the gate. "This court order says otherwise."

I don't bother looking at the document. I already saw what it said the first time he showed it to me. It looks legit and that's a problem, one I'm still trying to figure out how to solve.

"I don't give a shit what it says," I snarl. "We've got proof that she's not Sarah Lowell."

"Sir, I've seen the DNA results." He nods toward Fender, Joker, and Riker, who are standing next to me. "And I'm going to tell you the same thing I told them. Get a lawyer. I have to follow this judge's order and I have every intention of doing just that."

"I'm an adult," Trinity says from behind me. "Not some child they can just come pick up and take home."

"Sarah, you're not mentally stable," Bill Lowell says, speaking up for the first time. "You're off your meds and not thinking straight. The doctors are going to help you."

"How'd you do it?" I ask, focusing on the piece of shit calling himself a father.

"Do what?"

"Convince everyone that she's your daughter," I clarify. "You must have deep pockets to get judges and doctors in your corner."

Bill bristles, opening and closing his mouth several times before spitting out lies. "I don't know what you're talking about. Sarah is our daughter. We've done nothing but love and care for her."

"Bullshit!" Trainwreck shouts as he launches himself at the gate. "You took her from her family! You kidnapped her from the woods and made her believe she wasn't—"

"Stop!" I whirl around and see Trinity with her hands over her ears, tears streaming down her face. "Stop, stop, stop!"

Her words trigger a memory and an image of her crying out in her sleep slams into me like a freight train, threatening to knock me on my ass.

All eyes turn to her. Trinity struggles to catch her breath through her sobbing, but when she does, she straightens her shoulders and walks to stand between Trainwreck and me.

"I'll go with you," she says calmly.

"The hell you will," I growl.

"Trin, you d—"

"I'm going with them," she repeats, more forcefully, shutting down her brother's protests. She tips her head to look at me. "Can you please open the gate?"

"No."

Trinity's eyes harden and she squares her shoulders as she turns toward Trainwreck. "Tyler?"

"I can't." He shakes his head.

Fender steps around me and walks toward the shack to press the button and disengage the lock. Time stops, oxygen disappears, cold fury replaces hot rage as I watch Fender lock eyes with Trinity for a moment before she gives him a small smile.

"Thank you," she says, with a wobble to the words.

"Don't thank me yet," Fender comments. "Save it for when we get you back."

I stand there, frozen, helpless to stop Trinity from getting into the waiting vehicle. Helpless to stop evil from driving her away. Completely fucking helpless.

And enraged to the point where all rational thought leaves me. I react in what feels like warp speed, as if someone shot adrenaline into my system to jumpstart it, and lunge at Fender when his back is turned.

"Why are you doing this?" I yell as we fall to the ground. "How can you let them take her?"

"Greaser!" Joker's shout reaches me, but it doesn't penetrate the haze. "Stop it!"

Hands grab me from behind and yank me backward. I struggle against Joker but remain focused on Fender, on the betrayal coursing through me, feeding my actions.

"Let me go," I snarl, throwing an elbow back and catching Joker on the chin. "He can't do this!"

"It's done, G," Joker says after a second. His arms wrap around my chest, pinning my arms to my sides. "It's done."

Through my tunnel vision, I see Fender stand, anger matching my own in his eyes. He stalks toward me, but before he reaches me, Trainwreck launches himself at him, barreling them both to the ground. They roll around for a moment and then Fender pins the prospect beneath him.

Trainwreck's chest heaves and he tries to buck free, but he fails. Fender is bigger, faster, stronger, more ruthless. Trainwreck has come a long way since he began prospecting, but he's a far cry away from where he needs to be to beat most of us in a physical fight.

"If I stand up, are you gonna come at me again?" Fender asks, a deadly calm in his voice. Trainwreck says nothing. "Answer the fucking question!"

"I don't know."

"You better figure it the fuck out."

They both remain where they are for several tense minutes. Fender finally stands and Trainwreck remains on his back.

Fender glances at me and back to Trainwreck. "Both of you have lost your goddamn minds." He walks to the shack to close the gate while he's talking. "Do you seriously think I'd hand over Trinity without some idea of how to get her back?"

"You just did!" Trainwreck shouts as he rolls to his knees and pushes himself up. "The last time she was taken by those cocksuckers, she was gone for twelve years. We did everything to try and find her... nothing worked!"

"He's right, *Prez*." I sneer the title, disgusted with his lack of empathy in the situation.

"Maybe so," Fender concedes and focuses on Trainwreck. "But you're forgetting one pretty big detail."

"What?"

"Your parents didn't have the Soulless Kings as backup."

Fender's right, I know that. But it does little to lessen my contempt for his actions.

I yank against Joker's hold. This time, he lets me go, so I close the distance between myself and Fender. Riker steps in close to Fender and stares me down. I ignore him completely.

"In case you've forgotten in the last few minutes, the Soulless Kings just handed Trinity over on a silver platter to the very people who have spent *twelve goddamn years* destroying her."

Fender grips the front of my shirt and pulls me forward until our noses are practically touching.

"And in case you've forgotten, I'm the president of the Soulless Kings. I am loyal to the club and this family." He nods toward Trainwreck. "The *entire* family. We'll get her back."

Fender shoves me and I stumble backward a few steps. "How?"

"By doing what we always do... whatever the hell it takes."

CHAPTER FOURTEEN

You check off all my boxes. You're young, beautiful. Everything about you is... perfect.

Trinity

"This is for your own good, Sarah."

Seventeen. That's the number of times I've been told that in the last six hours. I don't know if they're trying to convince me or themselves. Either way, I don't believe a word of it. I may have a few years ago, before shit took a turn for the worse.

"My name is Tr—"

Pain ricochets through my cheek when Ma's knuckles connect in a backhanded slap. Pa quickly wraps his arm around her waist and pulls her into his side.

"That's enough," he whispers harshly as he glances around the parking lot. "What the hell do you think would happen if someone had seen that?"

Ma takes a deep breath and forces a smile. "You're right, of course." She fixes her gaze on me. "Sarah, honey, are you okay?"

Seriously? No I'm not fucking okay. I just gave myself up to you nutjobs and I'm putting my life in the hands of people I barely know.

I wiggle my jaw, as if to test the level of pain. "I'm fine."

"Now," Pa begins. "Let's stick to the plan. Get her checked in and after a few days, we'll pick her up and get back to business as usual."

"Business as usual?"

I immediately want to call the question back, suck it up and swallow it until my stomach acid dissolves it. Too bad that's not how words work.

"Yes, business as usual," he confirms. "Your little stunt cost us our newest, and most powerful client. Fortunately, he's a doctor." Pa holds up his copy of the court order. "He was more than willing to help us convince a judge you have a screw loose and need to be under his care. For a price, of course. One you're going to be spending a lot of time and effort earning."

"Sarah, really." Ma lifts my hands and pulls them to her chest. I cringe at her touch but force myself to play along. "What were you thinking, climbing out a bathroom window?"

"I was thinking I wanted to get my life back."

"Well, now you've seen how well that worked out for you." Pa opens the trunk and pulls out a duffel bag. He slings it over his shoulder and nods toward the door of the hospital. "Let's get you inside."

They flank me, both of their hands on my back, urging me forward. I try to pull away from them, but they don't allow it. My eyes fixate on the small sign next to the door. *Greener Pastures Psychiatric Facility.* I've never heard of it, but that doesn't mean anything. In the past, when Ma and Pa enlisted the help of doctors to keep me in line, one always came to the house. Having me committed is new.

"Welcome to Greener Pastures."

I lift my head and stare at the woman behind a reception desk. I look around the lobby, taking in the upscale decor, and some of my tension eases. Maybe this won't be as bad as I thought. This place feels more like a spa than a mental hospital. Surely I can make it through until the Soulless Kings come for me.

If they come for you.

"Hello, Miss..." Ma stretches her arm out to shake the woman's hand.

"Cordell. Sandra Cordell."

"Nice to meet you, Sandra." Ma says and glances at Pa while she pulls me forward. "We're Eileen and Bill Lowell, and this is our daughter, Sarah."

Sandra smiles broadly and looks down at her desk. "Ah, yes." She lifts a folder. "Dr. Masters is expecting you."

A man walks through the door behind the reception area. His eyes slide from Ma and Pa to me then travel the length of my body. He licks his lips and disgust smacks me in the face.

"I'll take it from here, Sandra," he says and walks around the desk toward me. His grin widens and he arches a brow. "We've got a lot of work to do, Sarah."

My commitment to biding my time, to playing a part while I wait for the Soulless Kings snaps.

"My name. Is. Trinity!" I scream as I swing my leg up, connecting with the good doctor's crotch.

Satisfaction rolls through me at his howl in pain as he falls to the floor. My actions catch Ma and Pa off guard, and I tear away from them to bolt for the door.

"Lock it down!" Dr. Masters shouts.

Just as I reach for the door to push it open, an alarm bell shrieks and the locks click into place. I'm trapped. I whirl around and press my back to the glass, my chest heaving, my eyes wide as I watch several men dressed in scrubs rush toward me.

I do everything I can to stop them from touching me. I kick, I punch, I scream. I manage to hold them off for a few brief moments and then a prick in my neck stops me in my tracks. Something cold slithers through my veins as my vision blurs.

My legs give out and I find the inner strength to brace myself for a fall that never comes. Arms scoop me up and fingers brush my hair back.

"You're going to pay for that." Hot breath crawls over my skin like a million tiny spiders. "*Sarah.*"

∼

"Well, well, well…"

I groan as I roll to my side, away from the voice. I hit something solid and force my eyes open to see what it is. My vision is blurry, so I squint to try and bring it into focus. A wall?

"It's for your own protection."

I glance over my shoulder and see Dr. Masters leaning against the opposite wall. Holy shit… it's a padded wall. They put me in a fucking padded room!

I open my mouth to tell him to go to hell, but nothing comes out. My lips are bone-dry. I try to make my tongue work to produce saliva, but it keeps sticking to the roof of my mouth.

"I'll get you some water in a minute," he says as he pushes off the wall and stalks toward me. "First, you need to know how this is going to work."

I scoot back into the corner, wincing when the cot mattress dips with his weight.

"I shelled out good money for you the first time around, and I'm going to collect." His grin is sinister. "It was just pure dumb luck that I got pulled over for speeding on my way to the motel. Pretty hefty ticket too." He shrugs. "But it turns out, your parents are not only paying for that ticket, but they also offered you to me free of charge… for a week."

Dr. Masters lifts his arm and stretches it toward me, but he drops it when I flinch and his grin slips.

"Here's the thing," he begins and locks eyes with me. "I know the Lowells are scum. I know you're probably not theirs to offer." He shrugs. "But I don't particularly care. You check off all my boxes." This time when he reaches out, his hand cups my cheek. "You're young, beautiful."

He trails a finger over my lips, my chin, down to the neck of my shirt and I can't stop my mewling protest. I squeeze my eyes shut as he grips my tee and tears it down the middle, the sound of ripping fabric scratching my brain like fingernails on a chalkboard.

"Everything about you is…" He palms my breasts and flicks a thumb over my nipples through my bra. "Perfect." His hands fall away, and my eyes flutter open in time to see his hand come toward my throat. When he latches on, pressing against my windpipe, I claw at him as I try to suck in air. "Except your defiance," he snarls. "I could do without that."

As quickly as it all began, he lets me go and rises from the cot. I watch as he walks casually toward the door and presses his thumb into a lock pad under the knob. The sound of a lock disengaging taunts me because I know I can't leave. Not yet.

Dr. Masters glances over his shoulder, and his grin is terrifying.

"I'll have one of the nurses bring you some water. Be sure to drink it all and get some rest."

He steps outside the room and closes the door behind him, but I can still hear his final words as he yells them through the barrier with his face pressed up against the small glass panel in the door.

"You're going to need it."

CHAPTER FIFTEEN

Is that what this is, why I feel this foreign sense of protectiveness, why I tried to drown in a bottle?

Greaser

Three days later...

"Don't make me break the door down, G!"

I lift the bottle of Jack Daniels in my hand, and when I see it's empty, I throw it at my living room wall. Joker has been banging on my door for several minutes, threatening to break it down, when he and I both know he has a key. Motherfucker better not break my door because in my current state, I'm likely to break him as a result.

I push off the couch and make my way to the kitchen cupboard where I keep my liquor, silently praying I have some left. I hear my front door open behind me and can't stop the smirk that plays on my lips. I knew he wouldn't 'break the door down'.

"You trying to drink yourself into an early grave?" Joker asks when leans against the counter next to me.

I twist off the cap on my last bottle of booze and tip it to my lips only to have Joker snatch it from my hand and pour it down the kitchen sink. I watch him do it, begging my hands to stop him, but I'm too drunk.

"Here." He thrusts a joint at me. "Smoke this. It'll help more than any amount of alcohol will."

"What are you doing here?" I demand as I try to light the fucking thing.

When it catches, I puff on it several times to keep it lit. After inhaling, I hold the smoke in my lungs and wait for the high to take hold.

"You missed church."

"What?" I say on an exhale. "Church isn't until tomorrow morning."

"Jesus," he mumbles and yanks the joint out of my hand to hit it himself.

I glare at him and for the first time since he walked in, I notice his hands are covered in dried blood, as are his clothes.

"What the fuck happened to you?"

"Like I said, you missed church," he replies. "Which means, you also missed the bloodbath in the Nightmare Room that immediately followed."

"But that's not until tomo—"

"Tomorrow morning," he finishes for me. "Yeah, you already said that." He shakes his head and pushes off the counter. "Get your shit together, brother. It is tomorrow fucking morning."

I reach for my phone in my back pocket and tap the screen. Shit. He's right. I scrub a hand over my face and groan.

"Yeah, you missed it. I tried to cover for you, but Fender

wasn't having it." He pulls a chair out at the table and plops down. "He said to make sure you've got the cash to cover your No-Show fine the next time you see him."

I sit down across from Joker, and he hands the joint back to me.

"I take it David's dead?" I ask, nodding toward his bloody shirt.

"Oh yeah." He chuckles. "Riker had way too much fun with that one. Trainwreck too." He pauses and locks eyes with me. "You'd have been proud of the prospect. I can't wait to vote him in. He's gonna make a hell of a Soulless King."

I nod, not trusting myself to speak. I can't believe I missed it. After three days of trying to track Trinity down, following lead after lead only to come up against one roadblock after another... I really could have used some time in the Nightmare Room.

I take a deep breath and finally push a few words out. "Did you just come to gloat or...?"

"No." He shrugs. "Although that's fun too."

"Just spit it out, Joker," I snap. "I'm too drunk and tired to deal with your shit."

He leans forward and rests his elbows on the table. "Squirrel found her."

Almost instantaneously, I feel sober. Sober and ready to take on the world.

I jump up and race to my bedroom. I hear Joker's footsteps behind me, but I don't bother looking at him. I grab clothes out of my dresser and stuff them into a small bag that'll fit in my saddlebags.

"Uh, what are you doing?" Joker asks from the doorway.

"I'm gonna go get her."

"Yeah, not happening." He pushes away from the wall and knocks my stuff out of my hands. "You can't drive like this."

"Says who?"

Joker throws his hands up in exasperation. "Do you even hear yourself right now? Fuck." He starts pacing the length of my bedroom and I glare at him. "About four bottles of Jack Daniels, that's who."

"I'm fine." I bend to pick my clothes up off the floor. "I'll get a quick shower and hit the road."

"No, you won't."

I haul my arm back, but Joker manages to grip my fist before it can connect with his face. He twists my arm behind my back and forces me down until my face is pressed into the floor. He shoves his knee into my back to keep me in place.

"We're gonna get Trinity back, asshole," he seethes. "But we have to do it right. We have to do it all legal and shit. Otherwise, those fucks are gonna be able to take her again. Is that what you want? Do you think that's what Trainwreck wants?"

"No," I push out.

"Didn't think so." Joker removes his knee from my back and flips me over before he stands. "Come at me again and the blood on my hands will be yours, got it?"

"Whatever," I quip and cringe at my tone.

Joker only shakes his head at me and turns to walk out of the room. He stops just before disappearing around the corner.

"Get up, get a shower, and get yourself presentable. We meet with the club's attorney this afternoon to sort through the legal red tape."

For the first time in three days, hope surges through me, and it gives me the boost I need to get my shit together. I stare at the ceiling and think about what Trinity is doing right now. Is she still at the hospital? Is she safe? Hungry? Broken and bleeding? Is she even still alive?

We're coming. Just hang in there.

The second Joker and I step into the main room of the clubhouse, Margo waves us over to the bar.

"What's up?" I ask, leaning on the bar top.

Margo slides two beer bottles to us, but I ignore mine. I also ignore the shocked look on Joker's expression when I ask her for a Coke instead.

"What?" I snap. "You wanted me sober, didn't you?"

"Yeah, I did. Just didn't think you'd listen."

"Would you two stop bickering like a married couple for two seconds?" Margo slaps her palms down and glares at us. When she does that, we know she means business. Sure, she's not in charge, but we're not stupid either. "Anyway, you've gotta do something about him."

"About who?" Joker asks.

"Trainwreck." Margo straightens and pushes her hair out of her face. "He's, well... he's a damn wreck."

"I just saw him not long ago and he was fine," Joker says. "A little bloody from giving a beat down, but otherwise, he was good."

"Goddamn, sometimes you can be dense." Margo walks around the bar and we both turn to keep our eyes on her. When she steps up in front of us and grips each of our shirts to pull us down to eye level, her eyes darken. "If that boy is so fine, why has he been locked inside the bathroom for the last two hours, crying his fool heart out? Huh? Please, tell me how that means he's fucking *fine*."

"What do you mean?" I ask.

She pushes both of us and squares her shoulders with her arms crossed over her chest. "I've tried everything I can think of to get him out of there. Bangin' Betties, alcohol, weed... hell, I even told him I'd let him take a run at me if he came out."

I feel the smirk coming and I'm helpless to stop it. I try to control my laugh, but it doesn't work. "I take it he wasn't interested."

Margo smacks me across the face, and I can't even be mad. The second the words were out of my mouth, I knew they were a mistake. I deserve that slap. Shit, I'm lucky a slap is all it was.

"Of course he was interested," she snaps. "But he's too broken-hearted to do anything about it."

"And he's broken-hearted because…?" Joker cuts in.

"Because, you dimwit," Margo begins. "It's been three days since his sister was ripped from his life and he's afraid he'll never get her back again."

"But we're going to get her back," I tell her. "Hopefully within twenty-four hours."

"Has anyone told him that?"

"Of course he knows that," Joker barks. "He knows we're meeting with the lawyer in…" he pauses to look at his cell. "…ten minutes."

"Well, I suggest you remind him then because he's not acting like that's knowledge he has."

Joker and I lock eyes and I nod. "I've got Trainwreck." I nod toward the hall. "Head on into the meeting room and we'll meet you there."

"You sure?" Joker asks, his eyes full of disbelief. "You're barely sober. Maybe I should be the one to—"

"I'm sure," I snarl and walk away from them.

The closer I get to the bathroom, the louder Trainwreck's breakdown seems. A part of me thought Margo was exaggerating, but it's clear now that she was not. When I reach the door, I knock and get no response.

"Open the door, Trainwreck," I command.

I jiggle the knob, though it's pointless because I know the door is locked. Fortunately, the lock is a piddly push button lock, and it won't keep me out for long. I'd just rather have Trainwreck let me in on his own.

After knocking several more times with no luck, I turn back toward the main room but only make it a few steps before I hear the door open. I glance over my shoulder, expecting to see Trainwreck stepping out of the room, but when he doesn't appear, I take a deep breath and enter and then close the door behind me.

Shock washes over me, but I push past it to focus on Trainwreck. He's huddled against the wall in front of the shower stall, knees drawn up to his chest, covered in dried blood. It's everywhere… his clothes, his hands, his face and hair. Tears streak wet paths through the crimson and drip off his chin.

I let my gaze wander the small space, and I take note of the broken mirror and several holes in the wall. Based on the gut-wrenching sobs that were coming from him, taking out his anger on the bathroom did nothing to ease his pain.

I drop to the floor and sit next to him, resting my forearms on my drawn-up knees. I know I told Joker I'd handle this, but now that I'm here, I have no idea what to say. I've been drowning my rage in booze for days so maybe I'm not the best person for this job.

"Wanna talk about it?" I ask, deciding to take a simple approach.

Trainwreck swipes his nose on his sleeve and shakes his head.

"Fair enough." I lean my head against the wall. "Care if I talk?"

Again, he shakes his head.

"First, how much of that blood is yours?"

Trainwreck shrugs. "Not much," he mumbles.

"Good. Let Gibson check out your hands at some point to make sure you don't need stitches or anything."

Trainwreck flexes his fingers as if testing the damage. "They're fine."

"Humor me."

We both sit there for several moments, silent, brooding. The devastation Trainwreck displays makes my own emotions pale in comparison, and I start to question why I care so much.

"I need my sister back," Trainwreck finally says, his voice a little sterner. "I need my twin."

"We're getting Trinity back," I assure him.

"No, you don't understand." He drops his knees so he's sitting cross-legged and twists to face me. "I'll never have her back. Not really. Not the girl I knew."

I think about that for a moment. He's not wrong so how do I get him to understand and accept that the woman his sister is now is equal to the girl he lost at nine?

"Growing up, Trinity was the only person who understood me," he says and chuckles. "Which makes sense since we're twins." He shrugs. "I didn't have a ton of friends, wasn't the smartest kid. But she didn't care. And she made me feel normal."

I can't suppress the laugh that escapes and Trainwreck glares at me. "Sorry. But dude, what the fuck does 'normal' even mean?" He continues to glare at me, so I move on from my point. "Look... you're right. Trinity isn't the same girl she was at nine. But she's the same person, deep down."

"I guess." He shoves a shaky hand through his hair. "It's weird, ya know?"

"What?"

"I really thought killing David would make me feel better, but all it did was amplify my need to get revenge for what Trinity has been put through, what I went through, what my family went through."

"And you'll get it."

"Something tells me it still won't be enough. Killing the Lowell's can't possibly be enough."

"Probably not. But watching your sister live her life, seeing her happy and healthy… that can be enough."

"And if she's not happy?"

"Trainwreck, do you really think Trinity is going to come back here and sulk?" I don't give him a chance to respond. "Fuck no she's not. She's strong and resilient. She not only survived twelve years with her abductors, but she escaped and tracked you down. It might take some time, but she's going to be fine." I grin. "Better than fine."

Trainwreck narrows his eyes at me. "You like her, don't you?"

Do I? Is that what this is, why I feel this foreign sense of protectiveness, why I tried to drown in a bottle?

Yes.

"Yeah, I do."

"Why?"

And there's the million-dollar question.

"Fuck if I know."

Trainwreck laughs for the first time since I entered the bathroom.

"Listen, the attorney is probably already here, and we need to talk with him, figure out what our next step is so we can get Trinity back. Joker told me Squirrel tracked her down so hopefully we'll have her home tonight… tomorrow at the latest."

Trainwreck launches to his feet and reaches for the door. "What are we waiting for?"

"I was waiting for you to get your emotions in check. If I've learned one thing over the years, it's that emotions have no place in a job. And whether you like it or not, getting Trinity back needs to be treated like a job. Otherwise, we'll fuck it up."

"No way in hell would I fuck this up," he snarls.

He would but it wouldn't be intentional. Hell, he wouldn't even realize he was until it was too late. But that's not what he needs to hear.

"I know."

"Yo, bros," Joker's voice comes through the door. "The lawyer's here and charging by the minute. Fucking prick. You about done?"

"Be right there," I call out to him.

Joker's footsteps disappear as he walks away from the door.

"You ready?" I ask Trainwreck after I stand.

"I was born ready."

I slap him on the back and chuckle.

"Okay killer. Let's go get our girl."

CHAPTER SIXTEEN

Toto, we're not in Kansas anymore.

Trinity

Dear diary. It's day four in this hell hole and I'm no longer confident in my decision to let Ma and Pa—no, Bill and Eileen—take me from the Soulless Kings.

A chuckle escapes past my lips and I roll my eyes. Maybe I really am crazy. Either that or I'm on my way to it. I've been mentally adding entries into a diary that doesn't exist and every once in a while, I catch myself talking to, well, myself.

I glance at the tray of breakfast food that rests on the edge of the cot in my padded room, my home for the last four days. It's been sitting there for an hour at least. It's brought in every morning before shift change, before *he* arrives. I shove it off the mattress and grin when everything scatters across the floor. I'm hungry but I'm also done. My hope is gone and there's no longer any point in trying to save myself.

Four days. Four fucking days of hell. It's been enough to break the strongest of people, but me especially. At least when Bill and Eileen had me, I sort of had a life. A shitty one, but it was better than this.

I swing my legs to the side and stand, stretching my arms above my head. I've only been let out to use the bathroom and shower, and I'm craving some fresh air. I won't get it though. I pace the length of the room, and when the sound of the lock disengaging reaches me, I stop and stare at the door.

Dr. Masters walks in, and his face falls when he steps on scrambled egg. He takes in the mess, and I watch as his shoulders tense up and he clenches his fists at his sides. He rolls his neck and when he straightens, he locks eyes with me.

"Clean it up."

I cross my arms over my chest while maintaining eye contact. He stalks toward me, and when the tips of his dress shoes hit my bare toes, he stops.

"Is this really the move you want to make?" he asks.

My heart is pounding so hard I fear I'll break a rib, and still, I stand my ground.

Dr. Masters wraps his hand around my throat and shoves me back into the wall. My breath is knocked from me, but I manage to refrain from struggling against him. His hand falls to his side, and for a brief moment, I think I've won.

The moment passes the second his knuckles connect with my jaw and my skull bounces off the white wall padding. A metallic taste coats my tongue, and I turn my head to the side to spit it out. When my gaze returns to Dr. Masters, his eyes are wide, and his face is bright red.

"Fine."

Dr. Masters presses his arm across my chest to hold me in place. He reaches into his pocket and pulls out a syringe, which triggers my fight response. I strain against him, struggle to get away, but he's too strong for my tired body. He bites off the cap and stabs a needle into my neck.

I wait for consciousness to leave me, but it doesn't. My mind races, my vision remains focused, but my muscles give out. Dr. Masters bends to lift me in his arms, and I scream at my limbs to move but they don't.

What the hell?

"Remember, we could have done this the easy way," he whispers in my ear when he lays me down on the cot. "But you didn't listen."

I try to kick at him, to swing my arms, but... they don't move. My brain is shouting commands, but my muscles refuse to respond. Dr. Masters yanks my sweatpants down, leaving them around my ankles. Next he rips my panties off my body.

"Take your shirt off," he demands before throwing his head back in a laugh. "Oh, right. You can't."

He begins to strip out of his own clothing, and I squeeze my eyes shut. I don't need to watch to know what's coming. I wish he'd drugged me with something to knock me out completely.

Dr. Masters climbs on top of me. He runs his hands over my hips, down my legs and back up my inner thigh. He moves so he's straddling me, and I mentally brace myself for what he's about to do.

Greaser

Ten minutes earlier...

"Ma'am, you don't have a choice."

I keep my gaze pinned on the woman behind the reception desk, while my ears tune into her exchange with Officer Shell, who arrived a few minutes ago. Apparently, five bikers entering the facility with determination and murder in their eyes was too much for her to handle and she sent up the bat signal. Lucky for us, the club's attorney made sure all of our documentation would pass even the most critical of eyes.

"You don't understand," she responds. "Miss Lowell is—"

"Her name is Trinity Milford," Trainwreck says from his position beside me.

The receptionist squares her shoulders. "Right. Regardless of her name, she's halfway through her morning therapy session with Dr. Masters, and it would be detrimental to her mental health to interrupt."

The hair on the back of my neck stands on end. *Morning therapy?* I want to call bullshit, charge through the door behind her desk and tear the building apart until I find Trinity, but I can't. This has to be done right for it to matter. Merely taking Trinity away from this place won't solve the bigger problem. It won't stop the Lowell's from coming for her again.

"Ma'am, either go get Miss Lo…" Officer Shell shakes his head. "Sorry, Miss Milford. Either get her now or I'll have to go find her myself. And I'm sure seeing a cop traipsing the halls would be upsetting to all of your patients."

The woman heaves a sigh and depresses a button on her desk phone and leans over to speak into the intercom speaker.

"Dr. Masters, I'm so sorry to interrupt your session, but there are people here to see Miss Lowell."

"Milford," I growl.

There is no response in return and her brows furrow. "Hmmm… that's odd," she comments. "He usually responds right away."

"Is there a reason he wouldn't respond?" Officer Shell asks, his hand shifting toward his duty weapon.

Her brows furrow, as if she's thinking, and she shakes her

head. "Not unless the patient became unruly and he needed to administer medication to calm them down. But if that were the case, there'd have been an alarm indicating he needed assistance."

I may not like the woman's dedication to her employer, her judgement toward myself and my brothers, but I believe what she's saying. More accurately, I believe *she* believes it.

"I'm going back there," I snarl and move toward the door.

Officer Shell commands me to stay where I am, that he'll radio for backup, but I ignore him. I'll be damned if I'm going to let Trinity stay in this place a minute longer. I can't do that to her, or to Trainwreck.

"Joker, go with him." Fender's voice barely registers the farther into the hall I get. "Trainwreck, you stay here with Riker, Piston, and me."

I silently thank Fender for that instruction because who knows what state we'll find Trinity in. Joker catches up to me, and we stalk from door to door, peaking through the tiny windows as we go. When we reach the end of the hall, there's one last door with a sign that says 'Employees Only' and a biometric security panel.

We exchange a glance before I lift my leg and kick at the door. When it doesn't budge, I pull my pistol out of my waistband and shoot at the panel, sending sparks flying, hoping to fry the circuit board and bypass the need for a thumbprint to get in. The door releases and swings open.

"Toto, we're not in Kansas anymore," Joker comments as he steps through the doorway behind me.

The hallway we enter is dark, unlike the front of the building. There are more doors, each one steel and each with a small window like the others. As we repeat our actions and glance in the rooms, my muscles burn. These rooms are padded and the patients they house are pressing their faces against the glass as if begging to be let out.

"This is a goddamn prison, not a psychiatric facility."

"G, this isn't like any prison I've ever seen."

"It's—" I stop in my tracks when I glance through the window of the fourth door on the left. "Motherfucker!"

Without hesitation, I shoot the panel next to the door and it swings open once the circuit is fried. I rush forward and grab the naked man who's straddling Trinity on the cot and throw him to the floor.

"Handle him," I bark at Joker before focusing all of my energy on Trinity.

CHAPTER SEVENTEEN

All I feel is safe.

Trinity

"Dr. Masters, I'm so sorry to interrupt your session, but there are people here to see Miss Lowell."

Ignoring the information, determined to punish me for my disobedience, Dr. Masters leans down next to my ear.

"I guess I better make this quick," he whispers as he reaches between our bodies and pumps his dick. "Don't worry... I'll go slow next time."

With his free hand, he cups a breast and squeezes... hard. He rolls a nipple between his thumb and forefinger and pinches, sending pain through the sensitive peak. I keep screaming at myself to move, to lash out and stop him, but I remain paralyzed.

Dr. Masters lines himself up and I close my eyes, expecting his thrust. It doesn't come.

A gunshot rings out and the door flies open, and relief floods my system.

Almost simultaneously, Dr. Masters' weight disappears and a familiar face looms above me. My eyes widen and tears form, spilling down my cheeks as I silently scream for joy.

"Are you okay?" Greaser asks, and when I don't answer, his eyes narrow. "Trin? Talk to me."

I can't! I'm trying, but I can't!

"Are you hurt?" His large hands run over my body, and I expect to be afraid but all I feel is safe. He traces my lip, my jaw. "The only noticeable injury seems to be here."

I blink several times, praying he understands I'm agreeing with him. My only physical injuries are to my face, but mentally? That's a whole other ballgame.

Greaser glances over his shoulder to take in the scene on the floor. I can hear Dr. Masters moaning and groaning, hopefully in pain, and realize that Greaser didn't come alone.

"Joker, find a back door and get him to the van," Greaser snaps. "We'll deal with him at home."

He moves to my feet and slowly pulls my pants up my legs, and after tying the string of the sweats at my waist, he reaches into his pocket and pulls out his cell and lifts it to his ear.

"We got her," he barks. "Have Trainwreck get the van and move it to the back of the building." He nods several times, and I wish I could hear what was being said on the other end of the line. "Got it."

He ends the call and shoves the phone back in his pocket before returning his gaze to my face.

"You're coming home, sweetheart."

I blink twice.

Greaser eases an arm under me to help me sit up. He lifts me into his arms and doesn't seem to strain under my dead weight. My head lulls and my arms dangle, causing him to try and adjust me several times into a position that's more comfortable. Finally, he sets me back down on the cot and squats in front of me.

"I'm sorry," he says, his tone indicative of pain, an emotional turmoil that he can't control. "Forgive me?"

I try to figure out what he's asking me to forgive him for, and the next thing I know, he's shifting so he can pick me up and sling me over his shoulder. My head and arms still dangle, but at least they won't catch on doorways and slow him down.

Greaser carries me out of the padded room and walks the hallways until he finds an exit. Sunlight beats down on us when we step outside, and the heat feels good.

I track Greaser's footsteps as he navigates the lot. Gravel flies as the sound of a vehicle grows close, and brakes squeal when it comes to a stop. A door opens and I see a pair of boots enter my sightline, next to Greaser.

"What the hell?"

Tyler!

"She's fine," Greaser says, but his tone is less than convincing.

I focus on the ground and the sounds surrounding me, and when Dr. Masters is dragged close, I squeeze my eyes shut.

"What did you give her?" Greaser asks, and his hold on me tightens.

"I… nothing," Dr. Masters whimpers.

Bang!

Dr. Masters screams in agony. "You shot me!"

"Next time I'll aim for something other than your kneecap," Joker threatens. "What the fuck did you give her?"

"What the hell is going on here?"

Who is that?

"Officer Shell," Greaser says. *Officer? Why would they bring the cops?* "What would it take for you to look the other way?"

"There's no amount of money—"

"There's always an amount," Fender interrupts. "Whether the price is money or something a little less... *legal*. Either way, everyone has a price. What's yours?"

"Are you trying to bribe an officer of the law to ignore a shooting and kidnapping?"

"Kidnapping? No one is being kidnapped." Greaser taps me on my ass. "You saw the paperwork. She was brought here under false pretenses. We're just taking her home, where she belongs."

"My question stands. Are you bribing me?"

"And if we are?" my brother asks.

"If you are, I'd tell you to rethink it. I'm not a dirty cop."

Bang!

The cop crumbles to the ground and blood oozes from a hole in his forehead.

"Too bad," Tyler says.

"Jesus fucking Christ, Trainwreck!" Fender shouts. "You just made this a whole lot harder."

"And you all were taking too damn long."

"I'll deal with you later," Fender says with resignation. "Joker, do what you gotta do to get the good doctor to talk. Greaser, put her in the van. And Riker, get Gibson on the phone. Maybe he'll know what drug would cause the paralysis and can tell us how to fix it."

I can hear Joker yelling at Dr. Masters and I wish I could be the one yelling. My body jostles as Greaser shifts to open the van door. He slowly slides me over his shoulder to lay me down. When his face comes into view, he frowns.

"Aw, sweetheart, why the tears?" he asks as he brushes them away with his thumb. "You're gonna be okay."

He climbs in the back of the van and raises my head

before settling it in his lap. He brushes my hair back before tracing the line of my jaw.

"This is gonna hurt like hell for a while," he comments.

Already does.

"Yo." Joker pokes his head through the van's side door. "Prick gave up the goods. Riker ran back inside to get something to reverse the effects."

"Good." Greaser's eyes slide closed, and he releases a long sigh. "Where's Trainwreck?"

Joker chuckles. "He's standing next to Fender, afraid to move a muscle. He knows he fucked up."

Greaser's eyes dip to mine and he mumbles, "Did he though?"

"Nah. Fender won't do anything. He knows Trainwreck was acting on emotion. We all would have done the same thing."

"Is the doc still alive?"

"Barely," Joker responds and Greaser groans. "Don't worry, G. I left some for you."

Greaser's head swivels and he looks out toward what I imagine is not a pretty sight. A grin spreads across his face. "I'm gonna have fun, that's for damn sure."

"You and Trainwreck both."

Silence fills the air until it's broken by a shout.

"Got it!"

Greaser stiffens and Joker disappears from my view. He's replaced by Riker, who's holding a syringe in one hand and a cell phone in the other.

"Gibson, I'm with her," Riker says.

"Okay, good. If you can inject the stuff right into a vein, it'll work faster."

"Give it to me," Greaser says and snatches the drug from Riker.

"No, I'll do it."

My brother appears in the back of the van and kneels next to me. My eyes focus on his movements, and within seconds, he's slapping the inside of my elbow with two fingers, trying to plump up a vein.

Questions plague me about how he knows what to do, but I shove them aside. It doesn't matter. Not right now.

"Trinity, this is gonna sting like a son of a bitch." Riker's voice comes through the speaker.

I don't care. Bring it on.

Tyler injects the liquid and Riker was right... it stings. But I welcome it. If it's going to free me from my mind, I can take it.

He pulls the needle out and rubs a hand over my arm. "There. Hopefully you'll feel better soon."

I blink several times at my brother, and he stares at me in confusion.

"She's thanking you," Greaser says, a smile on his lips.

"How do you know?"

"Because." Greaser shrugs. "It's what I would do."

CHAPTER EIGHTEEN

I'll promise this woman anything.

Greaser

"They won't let this go, let *her* go."

I glance in the rearview mirror just in time to see Trainwreck throw an elbow in Dr. Masters' face, knocking him unconscious. My lips pull into a grin. I wish I were the one causing him pain, but Trainwreck is the next best thing.

"Leave some for me."

Trainwreck raises his head and smirks. "No promises."

Shaking my head, I return my attention to the road. We were hoping to make it the whole way home but tying up loose ends took longer than we thought. Officer Shell may not have been easily bribed, but it turns out, others in his precinct are.

As it stands, we need to stop at a hotel for the night. I'm fine to keep going, but Trinity deserves to sleep in a warm bed, not a cramped van. It's been a long few days, and based on her soft snoring, she's exhausted.

"He's probably right," Trainwreck states, his tone full of disgust. "The Lowell's aren't going to be happy when they find out we have Trinity."

"I know."

"So, what's the plan?"

"For now, we make sure Trinity is okay and get some rest." My fingers tighten on the steering wheel. "Long term? We take the fuckers out."

Trainwreck gives a curt nod and leans against the side of the van. I drive for another thirty minutes before taking an exit that boasts several hotels. I see the Harleys behind me follow, and my eye twitches when I catch sight of Joker. He's on my bike because I wanted to stay with Trinity and I'm not crazy about it.

After parking the van, I reach over and gently shake Trinity to wake her. She flails her arms, and I put mine up to deflect. When her eyes land on me, her movements still and she relaxes in her seat.

"Are we home?"

Home.

That one word has always held a deeper meaning than a house to lay my head at night. For me, home is anywhere my family is, where my brothers are. It still is but now every time I picture home, Trinity is in the vision.

"No. A hotel."

She rubs her eyes and glances out her window. "Oh."

"We figured you'd want to get some sleep in a real bed," her brother says.

Trinity twists in her seat to look in the back. "What about him?" she asks and nods at the doctor.

"Joker's gonna take him the rest of the way."

She frowns. "How?"

"He's taking the van." I pull on the handle and push open the door.

"But how will we get home?"

"My bike," I say simply.

She sits there a moment before shrugging. "Okay."

I walk around the vehicle to talk to Joker, who parked my bike in the space next to us on the passenger side. I hand him the keys to the van, and he lets them dangle from his fingers.

"Don't let Trainwreck kill that bastard," I demand.

"I won't," Joker assures me. "Besides, he knows how badly you want a piece of him."

"Yeah, but he's a loose cannon." I glance toward the van. "Killing that cop was a dumbass move. There's no telling what he'll do with emotions calling the shots."

Joker rests a hand on my shoulder. "I got this, G. You handle her." He nods toward Trinity, who's standing by the back bumper, and there's a teasing note in his tone.

"Not happening, bro." I thrust a hand through my hair. "Fuck, she was almost…" The word dies on my tongue, and I shake my head. "There's no telling what she went through before we got there."

"And yet, she's okay staying in a hotel with you, alone."

I roll my eyes, not dignifying that with a response. I'd be lying if I said I haven't had some… wicked thoughts about Trinity, but I'm not a total asshole. I know when to back off, and tonight, I need to back off.

"Get outta here," I say to Joker. "We'll hit the road in the morning, as soon as she's up and ready."

I turn away from him and walk to Trinity. Joker goes to the driver's side of the van and climbs in, firing it up right away.

"Tyler isn't staying?" she asks.

"Nope. Just us."

"Is he in trouble for what he did back there?" Her eyes

dart from me to the van. "I don't want him to be hurt for som—"

"Sweetheart, he's not." I brush her hair out of her eyes before tipping her chin up so I can look her in the eyes. "There are times when our actions need punished because they go against what's best for the club. But…" I shake my head. "Fender knows Trainwreck is loyal, worthy of the patch. He knows why he did what he did. Your brother is going to be fine. Besides, I think it's punishment enough that he can't stay here with you."

"Promise?"

I hate promises. Other than the promise I made to the Soulless Kings, I try never to make them. Promises are sticky. They rely on everything happening in just the right way. They're almost impossible to keep because of it. But I'll promise this woman anything. Hell, I'd promise her the sun, moon, and stars if they were mine to give.

Why? You don't trust women. Shit, you don't trust most people. So why do you want to do anything and everything for her?

"I promise."

I bang on the side panel of the van to let Joker know he can go. We step out of the way to allow him to back out of the parking space, and when the taillights disappear down the road, I throw my arm around Trinity's shoulders and ease her toward the hotel entrance.

After securing a room, I guide her to the elevator and we take it to the fifth floor. I find our room, open the door, and follow her inside. She stops in her tracks when she sees there's only one bed.

"I thought we'd have two beds," she mumbles.

"I asked for two, but this is all that's available."

"Oh." She sits on the edge of the mattress. "I must've zoned out while you were getting the room."

She did, but that's okay. I know she's tired. Add in the fact that she's been injected with at least two different drugs in the last twelve hours and who knows how much her brain is actually tracking.

"I'll sleep on the floor," I assure her.

She lifts her head and locks eyes with me. "Are you sure? I don't want you to be sore in the morning."

"Sweetheart, it's fine. Don't worry about it, okay?"

She nods and stands to make her way to the bathroom. "I'm gonna take a shower."

Trinity closes the door behind her, the lock clicking into place within seconds. I make my way to the bed and flop down across it before toeing my boots off and listening to them thud onto the floor.

I close my eyes and focus on the noises coming from the bathroom: the water turning on, the shower curtain being drawn back. All of it shifts my mind to thoughts that have no business being in my head. Not now, not anytime soon.

I fling an arm over my head and groan.

It's gonna be a long fucking night.

CHAPTER NINETEEN

In less than a week he went from a frightening stranger to a person I need, to being my person.

Trinity

Shivers wrack my body as the water turns cold. I flatten my palms on the wall and brace myself on outstretched hands. I don't want to get out of the shower. I don't want to face the man on the other side of the door, face his questions. Because he's bound to have some.

I straighten and scrub a hand over my face. I can't stay in here forever, despite everything in me begging to do just that. Twisting the knob, I turn the water off, immediately missing it when it stops trickling. I slowly open the shower curtain and step over the edge of the tub.

It doesn't dawn on me that I have no clean clothes until I wrap a towel around me. Shit. Now what?

I swipe at the mirror and, leaning forward to brace myself on outstretched arms, stare at my reflection. My jaw is swollen and bruised and there are matching injuries under my eyes. Any more backhanded slaps to the face and I'd probably have a few broken bones too.

Tears spill over my lashes and snake down my cheeks to drip onto the counter. Pressing a fist to my mouth, I try to stop the sobs that are threatening. I don't want to cry. It doesn't change anything, it doesn't make my heart hurt any less. All it does is make me remember all the events in my life that cause the tears.

Being kidnapped at age nine.

Being told my parents didn't love me anymore.

Being forced to accept a new family, a new life.

Being shoved into adult situations, starting at age fifteen.

Being passed from one client to another to 'earn my keep'.

Escaping at age twenty-one.

Committed a week later.

All of it builds in my chest until there's nowhere for it to go but up and out. I throw my head back and scream, not giving a damn about where I am. I purge every single thing that I've bottled up for so long, all the evil, all the heartache, all the rage, all the fear.

"Trinity?" he calls out softly.

I double over and try to control myself when Greaser's voice registers. My chest heaves as I try to suck in air. My efforts are useless. He already heard me. Hell, the whole hotel probably heard me.

"Open the door, sweetheart."

I twist the doorknob to pop the lock, but I don't open the door. I can't quite make myself eliminate the barrier between us. Greaser has no such problem. As soon as the lock is disengaged, he opens the door.

I avoid eye contact, but that doesn't make the scorching heat his gaze is boring into me feel any less intrusive. I brush past him, ignoring the zing of electricity that shoots up my arm when my arm connects briefly with his, and make my way to the bed.

Greaser doesn't immediately follow, and I finally allow myself to look at him. He seems rooted in place just outside the bathroom door. His arms hang down and he clenches and unclenches his fists several times. I don't know if it's anger causing the action, but I *do* know I don't feel fear. There isn't a single part of me that worries he's angry at me or will hurt me because of his rage.

When Greaser shifts to walk toward me, his eyes are dark, focused, full of something I can't put a finger on. My stomach does a little flip-flop, and my heart skips a beat. I tell myself it's my body's still reacting to the multiple drugs I was dosed with earlier, but I know it's a lie.

"Are you okay?" he asks when he's inches away from me.

I swallow past the lump in my throat and shake my head, not trusting myself to speak.

"Are you still worried about your brother?"

Again, I shake my head.

"Wanna talk about it?"

I start to shake my head for a third time but stop myself because yeah, I kinda do want to talk about it. I don't know if I'm ready to give him all the details, but I can't keep holding everything in because I'm scared of how it will affect others. I need to share my struggles with someone, and right now, Greaser is my only option.

And as much as I tell myself all of this, words still stick to the roof of my mouth like peanut butter. Needing to do something is far different than actually doing it.

Greaser sits next to me, so close our thighs are touching. I'm thankful for the terry cloth and denim between us because having any sort of conversation with this man is difficult enough. Flesh on flesh would make it almost impossible.

"I have an idea," he says quietly.

I turn to look at him. "What's that?"

"Why don't I order some room service? We can eat, get some food in your belly, and then we can talk."

My stomach chooses that moment to growl and some of the tension surrounding me eases.

"I'll take that as a yes," he says and chuckles.

Greaser orders room service; burgers for both of us, fries, and a bottle of wine. For a fleeting second, I worry the wine is his way of manipulating the situation, but I dismiss it quickly. I can't say he's been kind to me from minute one, but he hasn't hurt me or manipulated me in any way.

"I'm going to wash up while we wait for the food," he says and shuts himself off in the bathroom.

I glance down at myself and remember that I'm still in a towel. My clothes are still in a pile next to the tub, and as much as I don't want to be naked, I don't want those clothes either. I walk to the closet, and when I open the door, I'm glad to see there's a robe. I throw it on and drape the towel over a hanger to dry.

While I wait for Greaser to come back out, I get comfortable on the bed and turn the TV on. As I flip through the channels, my mind wanders. I recall another time I stared at a television, in shock by the breaking news story that interrupted whatever show I was watching.

"Behind me you can see the devastation this accident left behind." The reporter presses a hand to her ear for a moment and her eyes widen before she looks back at the camera. *"I've just been informed that the two casualties have been identified as Wallace and Tracy Milford. If that name sounds familiar, that's because the Milford family made headlines nine years ago when their young daughter disappeared from a campground. Their daughter was later declared dead, but the case remains open as her abductors were never found."*

"Trinity!"

I twist my neck so fast at Greaser's voice it takes a moment for my vision to focus on him and not the images in my brain. He thrusts a plate at me, and when I take it, he grabs another from the room service tray and sits down next to me, his back to the wall like mine.

"You didn't hear them knocking?" he asks before popping a french fry into his mouth.

"What?" I glance at the door and then at my plate. "No, I guess not."

"Where were you just now? You looked like you'd seen a ghost."

"I… I was…" I take a bite of my burger to stall while I get my thoughts in order. After swallowing, I try again. "I was thinking about my parents."

Greaser's face hardens and his muscles visibly tense. "Sweetheart, we'll get them. They'll never hu—"

"My real parents."

His body deflates. "Oh." He eats a few more fries before continuing. "What about them?"

About how I found out they died.

"What has my brother told the club about them?" I ask rather than answer.

"Not much," Greaser admits and shrugs. "We knew his parents died, but he never gave any indication as to how. Shit, we didn't even know ab—" He clamps his mouth shut.

"About me," I finish for him. "You didn't even know about me."

Greaser doesn't respond. Instead, he starts shoveling food into his mouth so he can't answer. I don't blame him. It's awful knowing my brother never told anyone about me, but I get it. For years, I tried to convince myself my real family didn't exist. I never thought I'd see them again, so what was the point pining over them?

We finish our food in silence, both of us full of questions and neither wanting to voice any of them. When our plates are empty, Greaser sets them back on the room service tray and wheels it into the hall. He locks the door behind him, shutting us in together for the night.

"They died in a car crash."

Greaser's eyes lock on mine. "What?"

"Our parents," I say, dropping my chin to stare at my lap. "There was a car accident." I inhale deeply and close my eyes before speaking again. "The news said it was ruled an accident, but…"

Greaser sits next to me and rests his hand on my thigh, squeezing lightly as if to simply let me know he's there, that I'm not alone.

"They have so many people on their payroll. They can get away with anything." I grab his hand and he intertwines his fingers with mine. "They got away with me. They got away with murder."

"Who?" he asks, confusion in his tone.

And I get it. My thoughts are all over the map and coming out of my mouth in a disjointed way.

"Ma a—" I shake my head. "Bill and Eileen. The Lowells. The crash wasn't an accident. It was murder."

Greaser's brows practically touch his hairline. "I don't understand. The people who kidnapped you killed your parents, your real parents?" When I nod, he frowns. "But why?"

If I thought it was hard to say everything up until this point, the answer to that question is infinitely worse to admit.

"Because of me." I draw my knees up to my chest but don't let go of Greaser's hand. "It was a few days after my first escape attempt. They um… Bill and Eileen wanted me to see how easy it was for them to get to people I loved. By then,

I'd figured out that they'd been lying to me for years about my parents not wanting me. I'd seen news stories over the years about the search for me, about me being declared dead." I shrug. "I guess they realized they had to do something to keep me in line."

Greaser tips his head back for a moment before snapping his gaze to me.

"Wait… it was Bill with you at the funeral, wasn't it?"

I nod. "He really wanted to drive his point home. I either complied with them or they'd keep killing people. And getting away with it."

"Jesus," he groans as he scrubs a hand over his face. "Your brother… he doesn't know any of this, does he?"

"I don't think so and…" Tears prick my eyes. "I don't want him to know. I… just… can we just not tell him?"

"He deserves to know, sweetheart."

"I know, but I don't think I can take it when learns the truth and looks at me with hate in his eyes."

Greaser's lips tilt into a sad smile. He cups my check, brushing his thumb over my skin. "That's not gonna happen. Trainwreck will be fucking pissed, but not at you. Never at you."

I lean into his touch and slowly close my eyes so I can focus on him, on this man who went from hating me himself to being the one person in the world, other than my twin, who I trust completely. In less than a week he went from a frightening stranger to a person I need, to being my person.

"If it helps, we'll tell him together."

I lock eyes with him. "You'd do that for me?"

He grins.

"Fuck, I'm pretty sure I'd do anything for you."

CHAPTER TWENTY

She looks like fucking heaven.

Greaser

The lock buzzes as it disengages when I wave the keycard over it. I push the door open and set the bar I'm carrying on the little desk against the wall. I turn to take in the sight before me and my breath catches in my throat.

Trinity is sprawled out on her stomach on the king-sized bed, one leg curled up toward her body and the other foot dangling over the edge. At some point in the night, she took off her robe and it's balled up next to her. Her ass cheeks are on full display and my body reacts.

My cock swells, my mouth goes dry, my nerve endings tingle. I remind myself for what feels like the millionth time that this isn't the right time, but it does little to defuse the lust. The only thing that will help is to find release, even if it is myself providing it.

I strip out of my shirt as I step into the bathroom.

Shoving my pants down, I kick my legs free after locking the door. I turn on the water and step under the spray to let it cascade over my body.

The image of Trinity, naked in the bed, flitters behind closed lids, pulling a groan from my throat. I brace myself on the shower wall and drop my chin. I palm my dick as my imagination takes me places that should come with a travel warning.

It's been months since I had sex, since I felt the brush of a woman's lips, since I held on to female curves as I fucked my sins away. I've tried, but ever since Cora, no one has been able to push past my defenses. Bangin' Betty after Bangin' Betty have rubbed their tits in my face, grinded against my crotch, trying to elicit some sort of response from me, but nothing.

And then Trinity showed up at the club's gate. Despite my distrust and horrible accusations aimed at her, there was no stopping the visceral response my body had.

It's been too damn long without a woman. I stroke my cock, desperately needing to be buried balls deep in something good. My desire is so intense, it's almost painful. I quicken my movements, thrust in and out of my hand, squeezing, pumping, *feeling*.

My pleasure is over almost as quickly as it began. My spine stiffens, my body jerks. The orgasm tears through me, leaving me feeling spent, weak... frustrated as hell.

I wash up before running a hand over my head to slick the excess water away, and then I turn off the shower and step out. I wrap a towel around my waist and sit on the closed toilet lid.

What the hell are you doing?

Good fucking question.

Disgusted with my use of Trinity to satisfy myself, I dry off and get dressed. I leave the bathroom, and when I see her, still sound asleep, still sexy as hell, I stop in my tracks. My heart trips over itself, stumbling like a toddler learning to walk.

I have to figure out a way to be around her, naked or not, without busting a nut in my jeans. That's not going to be easy, especially when I have to drive home on my Harley with her plastered to my back, hanging on to me like her life depends on it. Because she will be holding on like that, I'll make sure of it.

I force myself to think ahead, to focus on the fun I'm going to have in the Nightmare Room when we get home. The pleasure center in my brain remains stimulated, but in an entirely different way. At least I've bought myself a little time erection free to wake Trinity up and get us on the road.

I cross the room and gently shift Trinity's foot onto the mattress. The scar from stepping on a nail stands out, white against her pink skin against white sheets. A fresh wave of fury crashes over me. This scar is the result of kids being kids, but what about the other scars, the scars that are unseen?

"Trinity?" I rest my hand on her bare shoulder and shake. "Hey, sweetheart, time to get up."

She rolls toward me and throws her arm across my lap. Trinity nuzzles her head into the pillow and her lips tip up. She looks peaceful, content. She looks like fucking heaven.

My cell rings, startling me out of my perusal of her, and I fish it out of my pocket. Joker's name flashes across the screen and I tap the green phone icon to answer his call.

"What's up?"

"Please tell me you're walking out of the hotel and hitting the road," he says, his voice tight.

I glance at Trinity and see that she's still sound asleep. I go to the bathroom and close the door behind me so I can talk without disturbing her.

"We will be soon," I assure him. "Why?"

"Well, for starters, I'm not sure how much longer I can keep Trainwreck from killing the doctor." Joker heaves a sigh and punctuates it with a chuckle. "He reminds me of you, actually. He sets his sights on something, and fuck if he's gonna be derailed on his quest to get it."

"Good," I snap, slightly annoyed at his description of me. "What else?"

"What do you mean, what else? That isn't enough reason?"

"You said 'for starters,'" I remind him. "That implies there's more than one reason for us to be on our way. What's the other reason?"

"The club's attorney called Fender requesting a meeting."

"Okay." I drag the word out. "And that's a bad thing?"

"No, not necessarily. But Fender said he seemed rattled, like something was wrong."

"Sounds about right," I mutter, thrusting my fingers through my hair.

"Look, G, we've been through a lot lately. All that bullshit with the Black Savages and Charlie, then my mom, Riley, and Holland... and we can't forget Cora. I get it. It feels like we can't catch a break too. But we will." Joker doesn't sound convinced. "We have to."

"How many more people have to get hurt in the meantime?"

"I don't know. But the quicker you two get your asses in gear and get home, the quicker we can do something about it."

Movement outside the bathroom door grabs my attention. The sound of a plastic bag rustling reaches me, and I realize Trinity is awake and found the clothes I bought her.

"I gotta go," I say to Joker. "Tell Fender we'll be there in a few hours."

I end the call, not giving Joker a chance to respond. Within seconds, my phone beeps. I glance at it and shake my head when I see the text from him.

Goodbye to you too fucker.

I shove the cell in my pocket and open the bathroom door to see Trinity standing there with her fist raised like she was about to knock.

"Oh," she says and jumps back, startled. She lifts the bag in front of her. "Thanks for these."

My eyes dart from her face to the bag and back again. "Don't mention it."

"When did you have time to go shopping?"

I wrap my hand around the back of my neck, suddenly nervous. "I didn't. I, uh, paid one of the hotel staff to run to the Walmart down the road. Told him your size and what to get."

Trinity pulls out the jeans and looks at the tag before frowning at me. "How'd you know my size?"

I shrug. "Lucky guess."

Next she grabs the long sleeved tee and hoodie. "Isn't this a bit much? It's hardly cold outside."

"You'd be surprised how cold you'll get on the back of my Harley."

"Oh, right." She shoves everything back into the bag and shuffles her feet. "Mind if I get in there so I can get dressed? I'm sure you want to get home."

I step through the doorway and brush against her as she steps into the bathroom. I turn around to face her, but the door is halfway closed by the time I do.

While I wait for Trinity to get dressed, I glance around the room and make sure there isn't anything that will be left behind. It's a pointless task because we didn't have anything but ourselves and the clothes on our backs, but it keeps me occupied.

When Trinity steps out of the bathroom, I whirl around, and my throat closes up. Well, shit. I thought for sure that my libido would be safe, but damn if she doesn't make jeans and a hoodie look sexy as hell.

"Everything okay?" she asks when I can't stop staring.

I lift my eyes to her face and grin. "Everything is perfect."

Trinity's eyes narrow, as if she doesn't believe me. "You sure? You're acting weird."

"I'm sure."

"So…" She brushes past me and goes to the door. "We should probably get going."

I glance around the room one last time. I tell myself it's normal to look around for things that aren't there, but the reality of the situation is I'm stalling. Because when I walk out that door, I have to get in the elevator.

After the elevator, I have to walk outside.

Then I have to straddle my bike.

And then, Trinity will wrap her arms around me and press herself into my back, and likely send shockwaves through my system.

So yeah, I'm stalling.

CHAPTER TWENTY-ONE

We all want the same things: to get my life back and make the people who took it in the first place pay.

Trinity

Everything is perfect.

Cars whiz past us on the highway, and with my cheek squished against Greaser's back, I replay those three words in my head. There was something in the way Greaser said them that sent a shiver racing up my spine. I stupidly thought the shiver would die once we weren't couped up in a hotel room together, but I was wrong.

So. Damn. Wrong.

Greaser's hand leaves the handlebar and rests on my thigh as he navigates a curve in the road. This isn't the first time he's done this since we got on the road. Each time, he's left his hand in place a little bit longer than before. And each time I find myself closer and closer to grabbing his hand and holding it in place.

I don't do that though. Instead, I pretend like his touch

does nothing to me, like it's normal for my insides to get all jumpy when he's around. I pretend that everything is perfect.

Greaser taps me on the leg and points at a sign up ahead. We're almost to our exit. And just that fast, my muscles coil with tension and my back stiffens.

The rest of the ride passes in a blur, mostly of me worrying about what comes next. My stomach ties itself in knots and when Greaser parks the bike in front of the clubhouse, I hop off and double over. My limbs shake, and my body convulses.

Greaser squats next to me and brushes my hair out of my face. "Are you okay?"

I shake my head, afraid to open my mouth.

"What the fuck is going on?"

I raise my eyes and see my brother standing in front of me, concern in his expression and blood splattered on his face. Bile rises up the back of my throat, and I can't hold it back any longer.

"I don't know," Greaser says as he holds my hair back and rubs circles between my shoulder blades. "As soon as I parked, she started to get sick."

"I'll go get Gibson. Maybe it's a reaction to all the shit she was given."

Tyler disappears and I focus on the movement of Greaser's hands. When there is nothing left in my body to expel, I collapse against him. His arms go around me, without question, without reservation.

We sit there in silence for a few minutes before there's a banging sound. I flinch and look toward the house to see my brother practically tripping over his feet as he rushes toward me, Gibson following close behind.

"Why don't you bring her inside and I can check her over?" Gibson says, his focus on Greaser.

When Greaser's arms slide under my legs, I stop him. "I can walk."

He narrows his eyes at me before nodding curtly. "Okay."

He rises to his feet and holds out a hand to help me up. I take it, and when I'm standing, I rub my mouth with the back of my hand. The five of us go inside, and Gibson leads the way to one of the bedrooms.

"Have a seat, Trinity," he says, pointing at the bed.

While Gibson checks my vitals, Greaser and Tyler stand by the doorway, arms crossed over their chests. They remind me of the guards you'd see at the castle in England and, despite my best efforts, I can't stifle my laugh.

"What's so funny?" Greaser demands.

"Nothing." I wave a hand in front of my face. "Sorry."

Gibson sticks a thermometer in my mouth and then glances at them. He chuckles and when he looks back at me, he rolls his eyes.

"Idiots... both of them."

"We're no—"

The thermometer beeps and Gibson looks at it. "No fever." He smiles. "Your blood pressure is a little high, but that's normal considering what you've been through."

"But she's gonna be okay?"

Gibson stands and turns toward the door. "Yes, Trainwreck, she's gonna be fine." He looks back at me for a moment. "You should probably try to relax for a few days, reduce the amount of stress you're under. But you'll be just fine."

He pushes his way between the two men acting like bodyguards and leaves the room. Tyler and Greaser exchange a look before advancing on me.

"I'll take you to my place," Greaser says before bending like he's going to pick me up.

I raise my arm to block his attempt. "I'm not going anywhere."

"Trin, you heard Gibson," Tyler says and moves to stand next to the bed. "You don't need any stress right now."

Annoyance flares and I stand up so fast they both take a step back. "You're both nuts if you think I'm going to be shut away like some fragile flower. There's too much at stake and it all involves me."

"No one is saying you can't be involved." Greaser rests his arm on my shoulder. "Only that it might be better if y—"

"Better for who?" I snap, shrugging him off of me. "Because I haven't had a say in pretty much every aspect of my life, so surely you're not suggesting it would be better for me."

I pace the small room, my muscles coiled tight, my heart thumping wildly. I know they're only trying to take care of me, but so am I. We all want the same things: to get my life back and make the people who took it in the first place pay.

"Don't we have a meeting with the attorney?" I ask, trying to move the conversation to what needs done.

Greaser shoves a hand through his hair. "Yeah, we do."

"And the Nightmare Room?" I lock eyes with him. "Isn't that where the doctor was taken?"

My brother steps between us, facing me. "Trin, we'll take care of the doctor. He's never going to hurt you again."

"I know he's not," I assure him. "But I want in."

Greaser shifts around my brother, so I don't miss it when his face hardens. "You want in where?"

"The Nightmare Room," I clarify. "Whatever it is you're doing to Dr. Masters. I want in on that."

Greaser practically shoves Tyler out of the way before bending to look me in the eyes. "No."

I stare into eyes that are dark, stormy, unrelenting. I should be scared of the man they belong to, but I'm not. Not even a little bit. I fold my arms over my chest and jut out my chin.

"Why not?"

Greaser huffs out a laugh, but there is zero humor in it. "You've gotta be fucking kidding. Do you see the blood on your brother?" he asks, pointing at Tyler. "Anyone who goes in that room comes out looking like that. Is that what you want?"

I shrug. "As long as I come out breathing, I don't give a shit about the rest."

The more I think about it, the more I want it.

"Okay."

Both Greaser and I snap our gazes to Tyler.

"That's not your call to make," Greaser snarls.

"You're right, it's not," Tyler agrees. "But what's the harm in letting her get a little revenge?"

"What's the harm?" Greaser shouts as he advances on my brother. "What's the goddamn harm?" He continues moving forward, forcing Tyler to back up until he hits the wall. "She could get hurt... worse than she already is. She could end up with lasting trauma from what she sees, what she does. Think about how you feel when you walk out of there," he barks. "It's great while we're doing what we do, but when the high wears off, it can feel pretty fucking shitty."

"You love the Nightmare Room and what we do in there," Tyler counters. "Besides, we'll be there with her so she won't get hurt." Tyler squares his shoulders. "As for the trauma... I'm pretty sure she already has that in spades. Jesus, Greaser, she deserves this."

Greaser looks over his shoulder at me and arches a brow. "Is this really what you want?"

"Yes." There is no hesitation in my answer. "Not only do I want it, I need it." I grin. "It's gotta be a good stress reliever, too, right?"

Greaser moves to face me. "Fine," he snaps, not sounding the least bit happy about it.

Without thinking, I launch myself at him, throwing my arms around his neck. He catches me easily, and after a second, his body relaxes.

"Thank you," I whisper.

CHAPTER TWENTY-TWO

It changes a person, shifts the very foundation they build themselves on, until they're unrecognizable, even to themselves.

Greaser

Forty-seven minutes have passed since I followed Trinity into this room to meet with Alan Forney, the club's attorney. Forty-seven minutes of sitting idly by as he reviews the DNA testing that was completed. Forty-seven minutes of hearing him talk about all the paperwork that she needs to fill out and the steps she needs to take to reverse the damage done by having thought to be dead for years.

Forty-seven fucking minutes of absolute bullshit. Trinity, Trainwreck, and Fender are holding onto his every word, but I've reached the point where I'm tuning him out.

"What about the Lowells? How do we stop them, make them accountable for what they did to her?"

All eyes turn to me.

"I vote for killing them." Trainwreck's words drip with venom. "They took her life, we take their lives."

"That's an option," Fender agrees. "A pretty damn good option."

"No, it's not." Trinity's voice wobbles but when she stands up, she looks confident. "I know killing them would make us all feel better." She chuckles but without humor. "I, for one, would feel infinitely better. But what happens after that?"

"What do you mean?" I ask, confused. "After they're dead, you can move on."

"Maybe," she concedes. "But there are others."

"Others?" Alan rises from his chair and moves to stand next to Trinity. "Others like you or like them?"

Trinity looks around the room at each of us. "Bill and Eileen have connections and money, but they aren't at the top of the food chain."

"So we go to the police," Alan suggests. When we all start to protest, he holds up his hand. "I know, I know. It's not your *preferred* method but hear me out."

"This better be good," I warn him.

"Listen, I did some digging. Trinity was declared dead, but the case was never closed because the abductors were still unknown." Alan digs through his briefcase and pulls out a stack of folders. He tosses them on the table. "That's every lead the cops ever had on Trinity's case. They weren't even close. Not only would we be offering them the closure they need on a high-profile cold case, but if Trinity is right, we'd be giving them a chance at some bigger fish."

"And that's good for us, how?" Fender asks.

"Do I really need to spell it out?"

"I think you do, Forney."

"Fine." He takes a deep breath and releases it slowly. "I will deny any knowledge of this but… the Soulless Kings scratch the cops' backs, they scratch the Soulless Kings'."

"It's not the worst idea," Fender agrees.

I lean back in my chair, my eyes focused on Trinity and

her reaction to the discussion. I'm not crazy about working with the cops, but if it's what she wants, I'll go along with it. My mind wanders to the doctor being held in the basement, in the Nightmare Room. Any doubts I have about this plan, I can always take them out of him.

"How quickly can we make this happen?" Trinity asks, wringing her hands.

"I can make a call today, set up a meeting with the detectives in charge of the case." Alan glances at his phone and taps the screen several times. "I've got a few openings over the next few days. I'll try to get something scheduled as soon as possible."

"That soon?"

"Is there a reason to wait?"

"No, it's just…" Trinity averts her gaze and focuses on her brother. "What if this doesn't work?"

"Then we'll kill them," Trainwreck responds with conviction.

She nods slowly and looks back at Forney. "Okay. Make the call."

Alan packs up his things, but before he leaves, he looks at Fender. "I'll be in touch." He's about to open the door and stops to glance over his shoulder. "By the way, I paid the guy you hired to replace Forge. He did great work on the court order to get Trinity out of Greener Pastures, and I wanted to be sure we could keep him on the payroll. I added that payment to your tab."

"Thanks, Alan," Fender says. "I appreciate it."

"No problem," Alan says before disappearing down the hall.

Trinity drops into a chair, heaving a sigh as she does. I move to stand behind her but resist the urge to rest my hands on her shoulders.

"Don't get too comfy," I say. "We've still got some work to do."

She leans her head back to look at me. "Work?"

"Yeah, work. Or have you forgotten your request to take part in what happens in the Nightmare Room?"

"What?!" Fender barks. "You can't take her in there. It goes against ev—"

"I need this, Fender," Trinity interrupts. "Please?"

"Gibson did say she needed to find a way to reduce stress," Trainwreck adds. "What better way to do that than in the Nightmare Room?"

"For fuck's sake," Fender mutters and turns toward me. "You're okay with this?"

"Not really." When Trinity opens her mouth to protest, I hold a hand up. "But if it's what she wants, what she needs…" I shrug. "Why not?"

"Because that's not how we do things."

"I tried that argument, Prez." I shift my eyes to Trainwreck and back again. "And I lost. We'll be there with her the entire time. I'll make sure she's okay."

"You know I'm standing right here, right?" Trinity blurts out.

"I know. I also know that Greaser doesn't let others take away his fun, so I'm curious as to why he's letting this happen." Fender grins. "I hope you know what you're getting yourself into, Trinity."

"I do." She nods. "Whatever happens in that room can't possibly be worse than the last twelve years."

"I wasn't talking about the Nightmare Room."

"Are you sure about this?"

Trainwreck blocks the steel door to the Nightmare Room

and hitches a thumb over his shoulder. I switch on the monitors so Trinity can see inside. She watches the screen, her eyes narrowing on the image of Dr. Masters curled in a ball in the corner. He's naked and his body is covered in bruises and lacerations. Dried blood cakes his face.

Trinity's eyes dart to mine, and for a moment, I think she's going to back out. Because the kind of revenge she'll get once she walks through the door isn't the kind that she can move on from. It changes a person, shifts the very foundation they build themselves on, until they're unrecognizable, even to themselves.

When she remains quiet, the tension in my body eases. I breathe a sigh of relief, grateful that she's come to her—

"I'm sure."

"What?"

My eyes lock with hers. Her pupils dilate and her nostrils flare.

"I'm sure."

"Once you walk through that door, you can't back out. You can't erase what you see, what you do from your memory."

"I know."

I heave a sigh. "Fine." I enter the code into the panel that will open the steel door. "C'mon then."

I step through, into the darkness, into the place where I feel most like myself. Trainwreck steps in next, coming to stand beside me, and Trinity enters last, coming to a stop on my other side. The lights flick on, and I look over my shoulder to see Joker standing outside as the door slides closed.

"Who's there?" Dr. Masters calls out.

I advance on him and bend down to grab the knife I keep in my boot. The light glints off the blade, and I twist it around in my fingers, letting the sheen center me. Images flash in my mind of all the things I'm going to do to this man, all the places on his body I'm going to thrust the blade.

Dr. Masters scoots toward the wall and uses it to leverage himself up. He struggles to stay upright, and Trinity rushes forward to steady him.

"You know that's not how revenge works, right?" I ask, slightly confused by her actions.

"Maybe not for you," she says and shrugs. "But it's how I'm going to get mine."

Trinity turns to Dr. Masters, and seemingly oblivious to the fact that he's naked, leans close to him. A grin spreads across my face when I hear her rage-filled caveat.

"For now."

CHAPTER TWENTY-THREE

He's just one sick fuck in a world full of them.

Trinity

"Did you just piss yourself?"

Tyler's voice registers at the same time something wet splashes on my pants and I jump back from Dr. Masters. As disgusting as it is, there's a part of me that revels in the knowledge that I scared this man so much he couldn't control his bladder. I latch on to that part of me.

"How does it feel to have no control?" I snarl at the doctor. "To know that your life, as you know it, is over?"

When he doesn't answer, Greaser lunges forward and wraps his hand around his throat. He slams his head against the concrete wall, and Dr. Masters howls in pain.

"She asked you a question," Greaser says calmly and lifts the knife in front of his face. "I suggest you answer it."

Dr. Masters stares at me, wide-eyed. "Sarah, you—"

Greaser's hand shifts as mine connects with Dr. Masters' face.

"My name…" I punch him again. "… is Trinity."

While the doctor holds his face in his hands, I glance at Greaser. His brows are high, his grin wide.

"What?"

He shakes his head. "Nothing. I just… I wasn't expecting that."

Understanding settles over me. "You thought I'd come in here, see some blood and run in the other direction."

"Well, yeah."

"Dude, Trin always had a temper." Greaser and I turn toward Tyler, and he shrugs. "It's true. You were a brat at nine. I learned never to underestimate you."

"Thanks," I say but it comes out sounding like a question. I'm not sure if I should be flattered or pissed off.

"I stand corrected," Greaser says. He steps away from me and sweeps his hand out toward Dr. Masters. "Proceed."

I return my attention to the reason we're all here. I put Greaser and my brother out of my head, focus on Dr. Masters and all the ways I want to make him pay. But first, there are a few questions I need answers to, answers that could make or break our ability to scratch the backs of the police.

"How did the Lowells find you?"

Dr. Masters narrows his eyes, but he also relaxes slightly. "They didn't."

"I don't understand."

"I found them."

"How?" His eyes dart from me to the men behind me. I grip his chin and force him to face me. "They don't matter."

"That knife says otherwise," he snaps.

I drop my arm and whirl around to hold my hand out to Greaser. Without hesitation, he hands me the knife. I curl my fingers around the handle for a moment before turning on my heel and thrusting it into Dr. Masters' stomach.

I pull his head toward me until my mouth is close to his ear. "They. Don't. Matter."

I yank the blade out and shove him to the floor. Satisfaction swirls in my veins as I watch him curl in on himself. I kneel on the floor next to him.

"How did you find them?" He groans in pain but doesn't respond. "You can keep it all to yourself, but you'll die from blood loss." I hitch a thumb over my shoulder. "Tell me what I want, and I'll tell them to save you."

"You're lying."

I shrug. "Is that a chance you're willing to take?"

He seems to think about it and the longer he thinks, the more blood pools around him. The thing is, he's not wrong. Of course I'm lying. But I need him alive a little while longer.

"Th-there's a w-website," he stutters. I press my hand to the wound to stop the bleeding. "There are lots of them, if you know what to look for."

"Go on."

"It's like a dating site but for people like me."

"People like you?"

"People with... *specific* tastes."

"That doesn't make sense." I shake my head as if that will make the pieces shift into place. "The Lowells took me at nine, but I wasn't matched until years later."

"At the time, the Lowells were new," Dr. Masters clarifies. "They were still learning, building their team."

Tyler rushes forward and kicks the doctor in the side. "Get to the fucking point!"

Dr. Masters tries to take a deep breath, but all it does is send him into a coughing fit, blood droplets flying out of his mouth. When he's done, he looks at me with imploring eyes.

"Can I get some water?"

"When you tell me everything you know." I redirect him

to the last thing he said. "When you say 'teams', what does that mean?"

"The website is like a dating site, but there's a twist. Each seller is a team. They build their team by adding people who can help them overcome any hurdles. Cops, doctors, lawyers, judges... name a profession and the seller likely has them on their team."

Rage boils under my skin until it feels like it's going to melt off. "What purpose does that serve?"

"Each year is a competition. Each product sold is worth so many points. At the end of the year, the team with the most points and the most income from their sales wins."

"Jesus fucking Christ," Greaser mutters behind me.

"What do they win?"

"I don't know."

"Bullshit." I clench my fists and dig it into the knife wound on his stomach. "You seem to know a lot about everything else. I'm not buying that you don't know this."

"I-I'm telling the truth," he pushes out through a pain-filled moan. "I don't know."

"Then what's in it for you?"

Dr. Masters tries to move away from me to relieve the pressure on his wound, but he has nowhere to go. "I can find what I want and there's no judgement, no punishment. I can do what I want, who I want."

I let his words sink in and realize I believe them. He's just one sick fuck in a world full of them. I can kill him, and still, nothing will change. Hell, we can take down the Lowells and nothing is going to change. There are others just like them, others who will replace them. There will always be more.

But maybe stopping one team will make the others think twice.

I remove my hand from him and stand. My brain is screaming at me to run, get away fast, because if I stay, I'm in it for the long haul and there will be no escaping the evil, not completely.

Then an image flashes of Tyler bent over to tie his shoe, of me peeing in the woods and being ripped away from everything I've ever known.

I won't run. I *can't* run. I have to finish this. Even if there are more, I need to make the individuals responsible for *my* suffering pay. I deserve that.

And the rest will follow.

"Stand up."

When Dr. Masters simply lies there, I take a page out of my brother's book and kick him. He cries out, but before I can do it again, he crawls to his knees, then up to his feet. He struggles to maintain his balance, and this time, I don't help him.

I press the knife against his throat, the blade cutting into his flesh until drops of blood trickle down. I glance down, take in the sight of him, and cringe. He's dirty, he smells bad, and he represents everything that's wrong with the world.

He needs to go.

"How much did you pay for me?"

His eyes snap to mine. "What?"

I increase the pressure of the blade. "How much did you pay for me? It's a simple question."

"Five hundred."

My stomach drops. That's all I'm worth? I recognize the ridiculousness of my hurt, how irrational it is, but that doesn't seem to matter.

"Five hundred dollars," I repeat.

Dr. Masters shakes his head. "No, you misunderstood. I paid five hundred *thousand*." The way his chest puffs out, he almost looks proud of that, of the fact that he could afford that price. "That was for the first time, the time you got away, and for an additional ten sessions after that. The Lowells paid me double to help have you committed and said I could have you, free of charge, for a week."

A million dollars. They paid a million dollars to get me back. I can't wrap my brain around that kind of money. Even before I was kidnapped, we didn't live an extravagant life. We had what we needed, maybe a little extra, but a million dollars? That's the kind of money dreams are made of.

"What's the name of the website where you found them?"

"Picky Daters… on the dark web."

I can't stop the laugh that bubbles up the back of my throat. It's not funny. This entire situation is fucked up, but really? Picky Daters? That's what they're calling themselves?

"How many others did you pay for before me?" Dr. Masters averts his gaze and I stick my thumb in his knife wound. "How. Many?"

"S-seven… seventeen."

"Okay." I take a deep breath, hold it for a moment before blowing it out. "Greaser, Tyler, I need your help."

They both step up to stand on either side of me.

"Tell us what to do," Greaser says.

"Hold his arms out and keep him pinned to the wall."

I lower the knife to let them do as instructed. I kick Dr. Masters' legs apart so he looks like a starfish, and Tyler and Greaser move their feet to keep him in that position.

"Here's how this is going to work," I say, smirking at Dr. Masters as I mimic his own words to me. I raise the weapon to chest height and thrust it into him. His mouth opens as if he wants to scream, but no sound comes out. "I'm going to stab you, over and over again." I pull it out and thrust it in about half an inch from the first wound. "Each time I stab you will be for each of your victims." I repeat the action. "Well, all of them but me. I'm going to get a different kind of revenge."

I stab him thirteen more times, each thrust fueled by rage,

revenge, a primal need to make him feel even a fraction of what his victims felt. By the time I finish, my hands are slick with blood. Splatters of the crimson cover my clothes, my face, my partners in crime.

I take a step back and admire my work. My hands are shaking but not because I'm afraid of what I did or ashamed of it. No, they're shaking because, aside from escaping and finding my brother, this is the most momentous moment of my life. I'm in control.

"I fucking hate you!" I scream at him, lunging forward and pummeling him with every ounce of fury I possess. "You destroy lives. You deserve everything I'm doing to you. I hate you, I hate you, I hate you!"

Tears pour down my face and I double over to catch my breath. I know Dr. Masters isn't the one pulling the strings of the trafficking ring. I know he's not the mastermind behind it all. But he's who I have in front of me, who I'm able to punish. For me, for other women like me, for society as a whole.

A hand rests on my back, and I shake it off and stand up straight. Tyler is still holding Dr. Masters upright, but Greaser has stepped between us. He cups my cheeks and forces me to look him in the eyes.

"Sweetheart, he's dead."

I lean to the left to look around Greaser and see that he's right. Dr. Masters is dead. He's probably been dead for a while, but I was too caught up in what I was doing to notice, or to care.

I shove Greaser away from me. "I'm not done."

"But he—"

I whirl around and lift the knife toward Greaser. "I said, I'm not done."

Greaser takes a few steps back, his hands held up as if he's surrendering. "Got it."

When I turn back to face Dr. Masters, I ignore the look on Tyler's face. I can't tell if it's pride or concern, and I don't want to know, not right now.

I glance down at Dr. Masters' limp dick. That's the only thing left to take care of. I lift it in my palm and swallow back the bile that rises up my throat.

"This is for me," I mumble and slice the blade through him until his penis is severed from his body. "Evil doesn't end with death. Now you can't hurt anyone, anywhere, *ever*."

Tyler moves away from Dr. Masters and lets him fall to the floor. He closes the distance between us and wraps an arm around me.

"You did good, Trin."

I nod.

"Do you feel better?"

I nod. And then the reality of what just transpired slams into me. My breath hitches, my vision blurs. I start to shake uncontrollably. I feel my legs start to give out, but I don't hit the floor.

"I've got you, sweetheart," Greaser whispers in my ear.

"What's happening?" Tyler asks.

"The high is wearing off."

Greaser tried to tell you this would happen.

"Get this mess cleaned up," Greaser demands of Tyler as he cradles me in his arms. "I've got your sister."

CHAPTER TWENTY-FOUR

If I'm going to hell, might as well enjoy the ride.

Greaser

"What the hell happened?"

I glance at Joker as he pushes off the porch railing at my place. I expected him to still be standing outside the Nightmare Room, watching the show on the monitor, but he wasn't. I managed to carry Trinity outside without any of the others seeing us, but Joker apparently went to the one place he knew I couldn't avoid.

"Exactly what I thought would happen," I snap. "She got her revenge." I look at Trinity's face. Her eyes are open, her cheeks are smeared in blood. "Then she crashed."

"Happens to all of us."

Images flash in my mind of Trinity stabbing the doctor. "Bro, you should have seen her. She was…"

"If you weren't a goner before, you are now." Joker slaps me on the back.

"What are you talking about?"

"I wish you could see the look on your face. Cora fucked you up and I get it, but with Trinity…" He shrugs. "I think you've seen how she fits in with this life."

"Watching her kill a man was definitely something I'll never forget."

"I don't doubt it. Just don't screw this up." Joker takes a step back. "She's Trainwreck's sister. If there is any part of you that thinks what you're feeling now is only a physical response to her abilities in the Nightmare Room, then walk away. Don't pursue it."

I want to promise that I won't, promise that this woman won't be changed forever because of me. But I can't.

"Take the tape of what happened to Fender. Everything he needs to give the attorney is on there." I glance at Trinity. "She's a force to be reckoned with, for sure."

"I bet."

Joker jogs down the steps and away from my house. I look at the woman in my arms and squint, as if that will reveal exactly what I feel toward her.

I carry Trinity inside and kick the door closed behind me. I make my way to the bathroom and set her on the edge of the tub. Before I can begin to analyze my feelings, I need to get her clean. I turn on the water, and while I wait for it to heat up, I methodically strip her out of her bloody clothes.

Trinity doesn't protest. She doesn't help either, so I know she's in a state of shock. I strip out of my own clothes and urge her to stand so I can lift her into the shower.

"C'mon sweetheart," I croon. "We're gonna get you cleaned up and then put you to bed."

Once we're both under the spray, I wash her hair. Pink-tinged water swirls around the drain before disappearing. I pick up the bar of soap and lather it into a washcloth. As I scrub her body, inch by agonizing inch, I try to think about something other than her naked perfection.

"I'm sorry."

I lift her chin in my hand and force her to look at me. "For what?"

"For causing so much trouble."

"Aw, Trinity." I pull her close and wrap my arms around her. "You didn't cause any trouble."

Her chin wobbles and she nods. "Y-yes I did. I... I ki-killed a man."

This is what I was afraid of. I didn't want her to walk out of the Nightmare Room and regret her actions. I didn't want those actions to change her, to make her someone she's not. Because Trinity is good, down to her soul, she's good.

"I know," I say. "But you also got some really valuable information."

She nods.

"You made him suffer for the sixteen others he hurt." My mind replays the moment she cut off the doctor's pecker. "You got revenge for what he did to you. And we're gonna be able to take down the Lowells because of what you did."

Trinity rests her palms against my chest and pushes away from me. When her eyes lock onto mine, my heart bleeds at the pain I see reflected in them. Instinct tells me to comfort her, hold her until the pain dissolves, but my conscience won't let me. It's not the right time. It's never the right time with her.

"Greaser?"

"Hmm?"

"Make me forget," she purrs. She tips her head back, exposing the column of her throat. Her skin shines under the water, and my cock responds despite me not wanting it to. "Make me forget all the ugly that exists... please."

I brush her wet hair off her shoulder, my fingertips tingling at the contact. "Are you sure?"

Wanting Trinity the way I do might make me a bastard,

but I've never claimed to be a good man. I've always taken what I want and as hard as I've tried, I want her. Now.

Trinity runs her hands up to my shoulders and pulls me toward her. Her lips press against my chest, and I'm a goner.

"I'm sure."

I bend to lift her into my arms and press her against the shower wall. My lips crash into hers, my tongue dancing along the seam, begging for entry. She opens her mouth for me while her legs lock around me.

For a split second, I wonder if I should stop. I tell myself to stop what's happening before stopping is no longer an option. And then she tightens her hold, pressing her wet heat against me.

If I'm going to hell, might as well enjoy the ride.

Trinity nips at my bottom lip, teasing me, tempting me in a way only she can. Her fingernails dig into my pecs, creating little half-moons, breaking skin and claiming me as hers.

I drag my mouth from hers and lean in to trace my tongue along her neck, up to her ear, flicking the lobe before whispering to her.

"Take everything you want from me." I rear back to look her in the eyes. "But know this. When you're done taking, it'll be my turn."

Trinity's eyes widen. "I've never taken before." A saucy grin spreads across her face. "I think I'm going to like it."

She lowers her legs, and I shift to let her stand. Trinity's hands roam over my body, as she circles behind me and turns the water off.

"Follow me," she says, and her words mingle with the sound of the shower curtain being shoved aside.

I turn around and my gaze zeros in on her ass as she walks out of the bathroom. I quickly do as she said and follow her, my granite-hard dick leading the way. She turns into my bedroom, and when I step inside, the door slams behind me.

I whirl around to see her leaning against the wall, her arms stretched out above her head. Her tits are on perfect display, and her legs are spread just enough to taunt me into skipping ahead to where I'm the one doing the taking.

Don't ruin this for her. Let her have her moment.

"Are you just going to stand there?" she asks, uncertainty entering her expression.

"Not if that's not what you want." I take one step forward. "Tell me what you want."

Trinity pushes off the wall and brushes past me. I turn to watch her crawl onto the bed, her ass in the air. A groan rumbles from me, and I move to join her. I flip her onto her back and lean forward. I fuse my lips to hers, kiss her until I'm almost out of breath and need to pull back.

"Tell." Kiss. "Me." Nip. "What." Kiss. "You." Nip. "Want."

"You," she moans. "I want you."

I roll onto my back, shifting her to straddle me as I do. "Then take me."

Trinity sucks her bottom lip between her teeth and looks down at my cock. Her nostrils flair, and her pretty pink nipples harden. Tentatively, she wraps her hand around my length and strokes. Up, down, up, down.

I keep my gaze trained on her face, the way her expression changes with each pump. I want to watch what she's doing to me, but I know the second I look, I'll blow.

Trinity rises up on her knees and slowly lowers herself onto me. Her eyes roll to the back of her head as she takes all of me. She rocks back and forth, her arousal coating my dick, and I can no longer be an inactive participant.

I press a thumb to her clit as she rides me, and I cup her tit with my other hand. I use my thumb to rub circles over both pleasure points, and her pussy clamps down.

"Take what you need," I growl and increase the pressure.

Trinity speeds up her movements and throws her head back.

"Look at me," I demand, pinching her nipple.

When she drops her head, she locks her gaze onto mine.

"That's it, sweetheart," I groan. "I want to see you when you come."

I grab her hips and start thrusting to meet her every move. We fuck like our lives depend on it. When her body tenses and her pussy spasms, I give in and let myself go. My cock throbs, pulsates as my release triggers every single cell in my body to explode.

Trinity collapses onto my chest when the wave is over, and I wrap my arms around her. Her chest heaves with her labored breathing, so I let her have a few minutes to recover.

Just as her body seems to settle, I flip her onto her back and lean forward until my lips are barely grazing hers.

"It's my turn."

I feel her smile as I kiss her, feel her give herself over to me in a way no woman ever has. And I breathe her in, accepting what she's offering. I want her, all of her. And I'm going to do whatever it takes to keep her.

I break the kiss and slide down her body, trailing my tongue over her flesh. Goosebumps break out on her skin, and her moans wash over me. I go over the edge of the mattress and kneel on the floor before wrapping my hands under her knees and pulling her toward me.

Her scent... the scent of lust, pleasure, sex. It's intoxicating, invigorating. I bury my head between her thighs and inhale deeply, and when I exhale, her body quivers from the sensation.

I thrust a finger inside her as I lift my gaze and watch her throw her head back. I add a second finger and revel in the way her hips buck against my hand.

"You're mine," I growl as I finger fuck her. "Do you hear me? You're fucking mine."

"I… yes, I hear you," she moans.

"Say it," I demand and withdrawal my fingers almost completely. "Say you're mine."

"I'm yours."

Fueled by her words, I bend to take her clit into my mouth, sucking on the bundle of nerves as I add a third digit. My tongue and fingers work in perfect unison, bringing her to the brink of heaven. Every second that passes, my cock hardens, begging to be inside of her when she comes. But I'm not ready to give up her taste.

I hum against her core and her knees tremble. Her hands fist in my hair and she holds me to her.

"Holy… oh…" she moans. "I'm gonna… ah…"

"Come for me, sweetheart," I mumble between her legs. "Let it go."

I flatten my tongue on her clit and practically slurp up her juices. She tastes like fucking sin, and I'm in awe that I'm the demon who gets to reap the benefits of it. I'm dying to get inside her again, but I need her to come first because I won't last once she tightens around me.

I flick my tongue, swirl it in circles, and her hips thrust up. Her pussy spasms around my fingers, her orgasm fills my senses. Trinity shouts out her release, and it seems endless. When her legs finally begin to relax, I know it's time.

I climb on top of her and grin. "We're not done."

Her pupils dilate and she smiles. "Okay."

I wrap an arm around her and drag her up the bed so she can hold on. I put her hands in place and move back to take in the sight.

"What?" she asks when all I do is stare.

"You are…" I shake my head. "There are no words."

"Oh."

When her smile falters, I realize she needs to hear the words. She needs to know exactly what I'm thinking, what I think of her.

"Trinity, you're every man's wet dream and then some." I trace a circle around her nipples. "You're sexy as hell." I trail a path to her pussy and tease her clit. "You push every single one of my buttons. You make me want things I have no business wanting."

"Like what?"

I line myself up with her entrance and thrust forward until I'm balls deep.

"Like everything."

At first, my thrusts are hard, purposeful, deep. But something inside me changes, shifts until my strokes become slow, torturous… meaningful.

What started as two people taking what they needed to feel good has become something else, something better. And for the first time in my life, I make love to a woman. I use my body for the sole purpose of showing her how important she is, how cherished she is.

I give Trinity my body to show her how utterly and completely mine she is.

CHAPTER TWENTY-FIVE

My heart is breaking, falling into pieces at his feet, and he's stomping all over them.

Trinity

Sunlight streams through the curtains, and I throw an arm over my eyes to block the light. I'm tired and all I want to do is go back to sleep. When I roll to my side, my muscles ache and I feel a twinge in places I'm not used to.

My mind immediately recalls why. Last night, Greaser and I fucked like our lives depended on it. A smile spreads across my face as I remember every second. What started as a way for me to put horrible memories out of my head turned into something… more.

I wrap my arm around the pillow and inhale. It smells like him. It smells like us. I briefly wonder why Greaser isn't next to me, but then I hear him. It sounds as if he's deep in conversation, but I don't hear anyone else, so I assume he's on the phone.

I swing my legs over the edge of the mattress and tiptoe to the door, pressing my ear against it.

"Yeah, I get it but…"

I heave a sigh when I can't make out the rest of his words and then it hits me. I'm being ridiculous. We had sex last night, so why am I hiding in here trying to eavesdrop? If he didn't want me to hear what's going on, he'd go outside.

Right?

I open the door and walk down the hall until I see him pacing in the kitchen.

"It's too much," he shouts into the phone. "I can't do this."

My heart thuds against my ribcage. Can't do what? Is he having regrets?

"No… yes… fuck!"

Greaser whirls around with his fist raised in the air, almost as if he's going to punch the wall, and he freezes when he spots me.

"Fender, I gotta go." As he pulls the phone away from his ear, he says, "We'll be there soon."

He stabs a finger at the device before tossing it onto the counter. I step away from the wall and walk toward him when all I want to do is flee.

"How'd you sleep?" he asks as he shoves his hands into his pockets.

I finally look him up and down and see that his hair is damp and he's dressed, ready to tackle the day.

"I, uh…" I shrug. "Okay, I guess."

"Good." He turns away from me and opens a cupboard to grab a mug. He fills it with coffee, and when he faces me again, he thrusts it toward me. "Here. Black, just like you like it."

I close the distance between us but don't take the mug. "Greaser, if you're having second thoughts, tell me now. I can't deal with everything else and also a rejection from you.

It's too much." I pause and take a deep breath but don't look him in the eye. "Just… never mind."

I whirl around to walk away from him but don't get far before he grabs my arm and tugs me toward him.

"What are you talking about?" he asks, his eyes narrowed in confusion.

"I heard you, Greaser." I try to force a smile but fail miserably. I swallow past the lump in my throat. "You said it's too much, that you can't do this."

Greaser throws his head back and laughs. Anger mixes with sadness. I'm glad he thinks this is funny. My heart is breaking, falling into pieces at his feet, and he's stomping all over them. Yeah, fucking hilarious.

He still has a hold of my arm, and I yank free before running back to the bedroom and slamming the door. Tears spill over my lashes and slide down my cheeks. I lick my lips free of the salty moisture.

I fling myself on the bed, burying my face into the pillow. I can still smell Greaser, and it makes the pain worse. How could I be so stupid? How could I believe for one second that Greaser would actually give a damn about me? He hated me. He wanted to punish me.

My only defense is I've never been in a relationship, and I latched on to the first person who offered me anything other than what I was used to.

The mattress dips under Greaser's weight as he sits next to me. He tries to touch me, but I shake him off. I don't want him to touch me.

"Sweetheart, do—"

"Don't!" I shout and flip onto my back so I can look at him. "Don't call me that."

"Why?"

"Because you don't mean it."

Greaser heaves a sigh. "I know what you heard, and yes, it sounded bad, but it's not what you think."

"Oh really?" I huff out. "So you don't regret last night? And saying you think you're falling in love with me wasn't too much?"

His eyes widen. "You heard that?"

"Yeah, I did. You thought I was sleeping, but truthfully, I was faking it because I wanted you to keep talking. I wanted to hear all the good things you were saying. I wanted—"

I press my lips together to stop my tirade. No use in revealing all the ways he hurt me. It won't change anything. I scoot off the bed and walk toward the door.

"Where are you going?"

"To the clubhouse," I say without facing him. "I'll see if I can stay with my brother."

"Don't you dare walk out that door," he barks. "You got to say what you wanted to say, it's my turn."

"Greaser, please don't do this," I plead.

His footsteps alert me that he's getting close, and when his hand settles on my shoulder, I don't have the strength to shake free of him.

"Don't do what, Trinity?" he counters and spins me to face him. "Don't tell you that you're wrong, that I am falling in love with you? Don't tell you that I meant every word you weren't supposed to hear last night? Don't tell you that being with you is the closest thing to perfection that I've ever experienced and that scares the fucking shit out of me?" He drops his arm. "Fine, I won't tell you all of that. But I will tell you this."

"Greaser, stop. You don't—"

"I'm not finished," he snaps.

If I thought my heart was pounding earlier, it has nothing on how it's thudding now.

"That was Fender on the phone. And yes, I did say it was too much and that I can't do this. But I was referring to having to tell you that the Lowells were located and will be arrested as soon as the warrant is signed. I was referring to the fact that you'd been through something pretty major yesterday, and I didn't want to add to it by telling you that we have to go meet with the attorney so we can figure out what comes next." He takes a deep breath and leans forward. "I was *referring* to the fact that I wasn't ready to burst the bubble of fucking happiness around us. I was in no way saying I regretted what we did or what I said."

"Oh."

Greaser begins to pace. "I mean, I was ready to swear off women for good. I haven't exactly had the best luck." He thrusts a hand through his hair as he walks. "And then you came along. I tried to tell myself you were nobody, that you didn't matter. I tried to keep my walls up, but they crumbled around me. Brick by fucking brick, they fell. Every time I learned something new about you, another one fell. Every time you looked at me, every time you breathed, another one fell." Finally, he stops and looks at me, his face a mask of pain. "I don't deserve you, I know that. But here we are. You threatening to walk away and me spilling my guts to make you stay."

"You want me to stay?" I ask, needing to hear him say it again.

"That's a stupid question," he snaps.

I cross the room to stand in front of him. "Maybe it is, but I need to hear the answer. Do you want me to stay?"

"Yes," he says on a sigh.

I nod. "I think I'm falling in love with you too."

Greaser's eyes light up, hope sparking in their depths. "Yeah?"

"Yeah," I assure him. "And it scares me too."

He cups my cheeks. "Then let's be scared together."

"Okay." I press my lips to his palm for a brief moment before saying, "Under one condition."

"What's that?" he asks skeptically.

"No secrets. I've had a lifetime of them, and I can't be with someone who's going to give me a lifetime more."

"Sweetheart, there are always going to be some things I can't share with you." When I open my mouth to argue, he presses a finger to my lips. "I promise I will never keep secrets about anything that has to do with you. I promise you that. But part of being in an MC is accepting that club business is club business, not your business."

I think about what he's saying, and I get it. I don't want to make him promise me things he has no right to promise. I don't want him to change or jeopardize his club, his family, for me.

"Fine."

"And you need to promise to give me the benefit of the doubt. No more overhearing one side of a conversation or a partial conversation and making assumptions."

"Okay."

Greaser presses his lips to mine for a brief kiss before stepping back. "Now, we have a little time to kill before we have to be at the clubhouse." He arches a brow. "How do you propose we fill that time?"

Greaser spends the next hour teaching me all the ways time gets filled.

CHAPTER TWENTY-SIX

They're all the proof you need that there's still good people in the world, even when evil exists, even when it slinks out of the shadows and tries to silence you, there are people who have your back, no matter what.

Greaser

Two weeks later...

"How's she doing?"

Trainwreck sits on my right while Trinity is on my left. We're in the pews of the courtroom, waiting for the judge so the bail hearing can start. Behind us, the seats are filled with Soulless Kings and their families, as Trinity has become as important to them as she is to me.

"She's good," I whisper to him. "Nervous, but good."

Trainwreck nods and shifts his attention to Bill and Eileen Lowell, who are sitting at the defense table. I follow his gaze and roll my eyes at their attorney. No doubt he's on their 'team' and the thought of what they're a part of makes me sick.

One thing at a time.

Trinity's hand tightens around mine, and I look toward her. Her face is pale, her eyes focused on the same people as Trainwreck.

"Breathe, sweetheart."

Her eyes shift to mine, and she forces a smile. "I'm trying."

"I know." I wrap an arm around her shoulders and pull her close. "You have nothing to worry about. The judge has your letter. There's no way they'll be granted bail."

"And if they are?"

"Then the Soulless Kings will ki—"

"All rise."

Trinity stiffens beside me as we both stand. The judge takes his seat and flips through paperwork that sits on his bench. When he's done, he lifts his head and stares out over the courtroom.

"Sit, sit," he says. Once everyone is seated, he turns toward the prosecutor and then toward the defense. "Before we begin, I'd like to remind everyone that this is a bail hearing. This is not a trial. You will each be given an opportunity to argue for or against bail being set." He leans back in his leather chair. "Proceed."

For thirty minutes, the prosecutor gives a bullet-point speech about how awful the Lowells are and the charges they're facing. He reviews Trinity's case, how her life was forever changed because of their actions. The longer he talks, the shakier Trinity becomes.

When the prosecutor is finished, the judge permits the defense attorney to speak.

"You're Honor," he begins. "The prosecutor will have you believe my clients are monsters when nothing could be further from the truth."

"You've gotta be kidding me?"

I glance over my shoulder and see Riley smacking Joker

on the arm, at the same time, the sound of the judge banging his gavel echoes in the room.

"That's enough," the Judge says. "If you can't keep your mouth shut, you can leave my courtroom."

The prosecutor shoots a look at us, and I mouth 'sorry' before making a mental note to take it out of Joker's hide later.

"As I was saying," the defense attorney begins. "What we have here is a couple who acted irrationally. I'm not justifying what they did, but I think we can all sympathize with their reasoning."

"I'm only going to remind you once that this isn't a trial." The judge leans forward, resting his elbows on the bench. "We're not here to discuss what they did or didn't do or why they did or didn't do it. Convince me they deserve bail... that's your only task today, counselor."

"I apologize, your Honor." The attorney flips through a file before pulling out a document and handing it to the bailiff to be given to the judge. "As you can see, my clients are hardly a flight risk. Mr. Lowell was recently diagnosed with cancer, and what you have in front of you is his chemo schedule. It would be foolish, and fatal, for him to skip bail."

Seriously? Cancer?

The judge narrows his eyes. "Do you expect me to believe that Mr. Lowell is unable to receive the medical care he needs in jail, while he awaits trial."

"Yes, your Honor, that's what I'm saying."

"I don't know what you're used to getting away with where you usually practice law, but in my courtroom, it's never a good idea to try and pull the wool over my eyes."

"Your Honor?"

"Sit down," the judge demands. "You've had your turn and now I'm taking mine."

The defense attorney sits down and has a whispered

exchange with the Lowells. They don't look happy. And they shouldn't. I'm pretty sure they paid good money for an attorney who will get them out of prison, and he's doing a shit job so far.

"Before I give my decision on bail, I'd like to read something to the court." The judge rifles through more paperwork and lifts several pieces of lined paper in his hands. "Ah, here it is."

"Oh my God," Trinity whispers and her hand covers her mouth.

"What?"

"That's my—"

"For the record, this is a letter I received from the alleged victim of the Lowells, and I'd like to read it because I think it is the easiest way to explain my impending decision." He clears his throat. "Your Honor. I would like to introduce myself. My name is Trinity Milford. Some know me as Sarah Lowell, but that is not who I am. I'm Trinity Milford and I was kidnapped when I was nine years old." He pauses and looks up to focus his gaze on Trinity. "I want it noted, on the record, that I see you, Trinity Milford. I see you and I am sorry for what you went through." He looks back down to continue reading. "I was held captive by Bill and Eileen Lowell until I was twenty-one years old. I would be lying if I said they beat me or locked me away or whatever is normal in an abduction situation. But they did silence me. They did do everything in their power to make me believe that my real family no longer wanted me. They took from me what was not theirs to take. And when I was sixteen, they began to show their true colors. I was sold to the highest bidder in their sick game. I was made a pawn in a much larger game, one I didn't even realize I was playing."

When the judge pauses, I glance at Trinity. Tears are

streaming down her face, and I pull her close to offer the only comfort I can.

"Your Honor, I escaped the Lowells. I tried when I was eighteen, and my real parents died because of it. It took me an additional three years to get another opportunity, and I made it count. I tracked down my twin brother. I found myself in finding him. But I found more than that. I found a home, a real home, and I found people who love me. Who really love me. You might be reading this and wondering why I'm telling you. And here's why. I'm telling you this because I need you to know that, despite their best efforts, the Lowells didn't break me. They didn't silence me. They can't. As long as I remember who I am, they will never win. But that doesn't mean they're not a threat. They are. Because they won't stop. If you set bail for Bill and Eileen, I'll accept your decision and do everything I can to protect myself. But I beg of you, please don't grant them bail. Don't give them the opportunity to do to any other little girls what they did to me."

The judge sets the paper down and folds his hands in front of him. He shifts his eyes from the Lowells to Trinity and then takes in the entire courtroom.

"Ms. Milford, I'd like to ask you a question, if you don't mind."

"Uh, yes, of course, your Honor," she says, flustered.

"The people here with you today... they are the family you found, the people who love you?"

Trinity swivels her head to look at each of us. She smiles at me, at her brother, at every Soulless King present and then she stands.

"Yes, your Honor. They are my family."

"And they will protect you, no matter what happens today or at the criminal trial?"

My stomach drops. This does not sound like it's going to go in our favor.

"Yes, your Honor. They will."

"Good. Make sure you hold on to them. They're all the proof you need that there's still good people in the world, even when evil exists, even when it slinks out of the shadows and tries to silence you, there are people who have your back, no matter what."

"Yes, sir."

The judge gives a curt nod and lifts his gavel.

"Bail denied."

CHAPTER TWENTY-SEVEN

So much for no secrets and promises.

Trinity

"Here ya go, honey."

I down the shot Margo sets in front of me and savor the burn as the whiskey glides down my throat. Slamming the glass on the bar, I wait while she pours me another. When I walked out of the courthouse this afternoon, I thought I'd be coming back here and celebrating with Greaser, in private, but the Soulless Kings have a very different take on celebration than I do. Hence why I'm getting drunk.

"I'm so happy for you," Margo says as she slides another shot toward me. "I can't imagine how free you must feel."

"It's going to take some getting used to, that's for sure."

"We'll help."

I laugh as Riley throws her arms around me. I've gotten close to her since the night I arrived, closer than to the other ol' ladies. I love them all, but Riley gets me on a level I wasn't expecting.

"I'm sure you will."

"I know there's still the criminal trial but having those two stuck in a cell has to be a relief."

"It is."

I try not to let thoughts of a trial, or the others out there who are a part of the same trafficking ring, get to me. I have to focus on the good, hold onto the good, like the judge said.

Riley squints at me. "What are you thinking about? Your mood shifted."

"What?" I shake my head. "Nothing. I'm good."

"Are you sure? Do you want me to get Greaser over here?"

I look toward the couches and see him puff on a joint before passing it to Joker. He throws his head back on a laugh and my heart trips over itself.

"No, let him be. He's having fun."

"And you should be too."

I grin. "I am having fun. Now, let's have another round."

Margo sets more shot glasses on the bar, and we down them quickly. I try to stop glancing at Greaser, but it's useless. If he's in the room, I'm going to seek him out. I've come to accept that's just the way it is with us.

With liquor coursing through my system, and my inhibitions lowered, I saunter over to Greaser. I ignore the whistles from the other guys and the protests from my brother as I straddle Greaser. When we got back from the bail hearing, I changed into a skirt and tank, at his request.

Greaser's hands rest on my bare thighs and he moves them forward, under my skirt until his fingertips brush my pussy. He arches a brow.

"No panties?"

I shrug and grin. "Nope."

He stands, with me in his arms. "Excuse us, gentlemen. We've got somewhere to be."

Greaser carries me toward the door, ignoring the jibes from his brothers. When he steps outside, the breeze blows my skirt up, exposing my ass, but I don't care.

"Where are we going?" I ask.

"Where the hell do you think?" He presses his lips to mine briefly. "We're going home, and I'm gonna fuck you."

"Sounds like a plan." I grin. "I'm free, so we can do whatever we want."

Greaser's eyes darken and for a moment, I wonder if I said something wrong. I quickly dismiss the worry though because he doesn't slow down or even say anything about it. It doesn't take more than a few minutes to get to his house, and when he kicks the door shut behind him, he shifts to shove me into the wall.

"If you don't want this, now is the time to tell me to stop," he growls before sealing my lips with a kiss.

Even if I wanted to tell him to stop, I couldn't. I grind against him and thrust my tongue into his mouth, imploring without words for him to most definitely not stop.

I work my tank over my head, breaking the kiss only long enough to do so, and fling it to the floor. I move to unbutton Greaser's pants, and he suddenly stops me and sets me on my feet.

He looks like he wants to say something, like thoughts are plaguing him, but instead he strips himself and lifts me back up against the wall. Greaser pins my hands above my head and sucks a nipple into his mouth to swirl his tongue around it.

All worry over his hesitation disappears. His cock presses against my clit and shivers race down my spine. I wiggle to adjust so he can enter me, and he releases my nipple. His eyes lock on mine and he smirks.

"I'm gonna fuck you now, sweetheart."

He impales me, burying himself in my demanding pussy. I throw my head back on a moan. Greaser's balls slap against my ass cheeks with each thrust, intensifying my pleasure.

I grab onto his hair, clenching and unclenching my fists. "I'm… oh God, I'm not gonna last."

He increases his speed, and our bodies stiffen in unison. My pussy spasms around his pulsating cock, and the orgasm zaps the last of our energy.

Greaser presses a quick kiss to my lips and lowers me to the floor. An odd feeling settles over me, a sense of dread.

"I, uh…" He thrusts a hand through his hair. "I'm gonna grab a shower."

He turns from me and walks toward the hall, and I rush after him. I manage to get in front of him and stop his retreat from me.

"What's going on with you?" I ask.

"Nothing."

He scratches the side of his nose, and I know he's lying.

"Bullshit." I cross my arms over my chest. "You were having fun until we got here. You looked like you wanted to say something earlier, but then you didn't. What's wrong?"

"I told you, nothing," he snaps.

"You promised there would be no secrets."

Greaser throws his hands in the air and heaves a sigh. "It's not a secret. It's just…"

"Just what?" I shout.

"You're free." He walks back to the couch and plops down. "You said it yourself. You're free and you can do whatever you want."

"Well, yeah. But that's a good thing."

"It's a great thing, Trinity."

I settle onto the cushion next to him and wait for him to elaborate. He doesn't make me wait long.

"You're fucking free, and I don't want to be an anchor around your neck. I don't want to hold you back."

"You're not."

"That's just it," he groans. "You can't possibly know that. You've spent twelve years living a life forced on you. I refuse to do what the Lowells did."

"Where is this coming from? You were fine earlier. *We* were fine. This doesn't sound like something that just popped into your head in the last ten minutes."

"It's not. If I'm being honest, it's—"

"If you're being honest?!" I shriek. "If? So much for no secrets and promises."

I stand and make my way to the door. None of what he's saying makes any sense to me and trying to figure it out while I'm drunk isn't gonna happen.

"Where are you going?"

I stop with my hand on the doorknob and drop my head before saying the only thing that comes to mind.

"Wherever I want. Like you said, I'm free."

CHAPTER TWENTY-EIGHT

If, if, if.

Greaser

"What the hell happened between you and Trin?"

I twist the wrench one last time before tossing it to the shop floor. I agreed to help out at Infinite Motors for a while, hoping it would be a good way to avoid Trinity and keep my mind occupied. We aren't open today, and I've had the place to myself... until now.

I stand and turn to Trainwreck, annoyed that he's here and forcing me to think about the one person I don't want to think about.

"Ask her. I'm sure she'll be more than happy to answer all your questions."

Trainwreck takes a step forward and seems to think better of it before stepping back. "Look, she won't tell me shit. All she does is cry. I'm—"

He presses his lips together and averts his gaze.

"What?"

He stares at me for a moment, as if weighing his options. To tell me or not to tell me? While I don't want him to betray Trinity, he better remember that I hold one of the votes about his patch.

"I'm worried about her, man." Trainwreck folds his arms over his chest. "She's not eating. When she's not crying, she's sleeping. And if the shouting is any indication, her sleep is plagued by nightmares."

A heaviness settles over me, as if the weight of the world is pressing me into the ground, unrelenting, unforgiving, unbearable. This is my fault. If something is wrong with Trinity, it's because of me and my insecurities and doubt. I have to fix this.

I grab my cut and my keys off the workbench and race to the front door to double check that it's locked. I turn lights off as I go, and when I yank open the back door, Trainwreck stops me.

"Where are you going?"

"I'm going to fix this."

Trainwreck steps outside, and I quickly lock the building before rushing to my Harley. I straddle the seat and fire it up.

"How are you going to fix this?" Trainwreck's voice booms over the engine. "You don't even know what's wrong."

"I do know what's wrong. I…" I shove a shaky hand through my hair. "I said some things that upset her. I let my own crap get in the way and she ran out."

"What did you say?" he asks, narrowing his eyes at me.

"None of your business," I snap.

"That's where you're wrong."

"Excuse me?"

He squares his shoulders and glares. "Look, I love the Soulless Kings and I'm loyal to them, to you. But Tr—"

"You better stop right there," I bark. "There should never be a 'but' after that statement."

"*But*," he says. "Trinity is my twin sister. A fucking sister I thought was dead. So yeah, I love the Soulless Kings, but she will always come first. If you have a problem with that, fine, take it to the others and deny me a patch. But don't for a goddamn second think that anything having to do with Trinity is not my business."

Impressive.

As much as I want to rip him a new one, remind him of his place and who he pledged his loyalty to when he decided to prospect, I can't. Trainwreck has proven himself to be a valued part of the club, of the family, and with that little speech, he's proven just how far he's willing to go for those he loves.

Not only that, but how can I be mad at him for doing whatever he can to protect the woman I love?

Trainwreck has come a long way from being a, well, train wreck.

For a brief second, I debate telling him all of this, but stop myself. I can tell him later. Right now, I need to get home and make sure Trinity is okay.

"Follow me home."

"That's it? That's all you've got to say?"

"For now, yes."

Trainwreck rolls his eyes at me, and I choose to ignore it. He's frustrated, he's worried, he's a brother. I get it.

The two of us navigate the roads home, going at speeds that make me even more grateful for the people we pay off to ignore some of our less harmful law-breaking. When I pull through the gate, I slow down to avoid rocks kicking up from the tires.

I park in front of the clubhouse and Trainwreck parks

next to me. I race up the steps, but he grabs my arm to stop me as I reach for the doorknob.

"What are you going to say to her?"

I glance down at where his hand is touching me and slowly raise my eyes to look at his face. "Let go."

"No."

"I've cut you a lot of slack because you're her brother, but don't think that means you can get away with anything you want."

"Answer me one question and I'll let you go."

I clench my teeth for a moment and try to hold on to my tenuous grip on my sanity. "What?"

"Do you love her?"

"*What?*" I snap.

Trainwreck rolls his eyes. "It's a pretty simple question, Greaser. Do. You. Love. Her?"

"Of course I do," I respond with no hesitation.

"Why?" Trainwreck's shoulders relax. "You barely know her."

"I know everything I need to know."

"Then why did you send her away?"

I heave a sigh, my patience running thin. "You said one question," I remind him.

"Why did you send her away?"

"I didn't!" I shout, all control gone. "The last thing I wanted was for her to leave. I…" I shove my hands in my pockets. "I just didn't want to do to her what the Lowells did. I wanted her to know she has a choice about how she lives her life, and if she didn't want it to be with me, that's fine."

"But it's not fine, is it?"

"Fuck no, it's not fine. I love her. I want to be with her."

Trainwreck pushes past me into the clubhouse and calls over his shoulder. "Then why are you still out there?"

He disappears into the bar area, and I hear him being

greeted by a few of the other brothers. When I walk inside, I see a Bangin' Betty sidle up to him, but he dismisses her. A frown pulls my lips down because Trainwreck has always given himself way too much credit with the ladies and it's not like him to send one away.

Trinity is having an effect on us all.

I stride toward the room that Trainwreck uses when he stays at the clubhouse and find the door closed and locked. I knock several times, but there's no answer.

"Trinity," I call out. "C'mon. Open the door." Still nothing. "Look, I just want to make sure you're okay and then I'll leave you alone."

"She's not in there."

I whirl around and see Riley leaning against the wall. She straightens, her arms crossed over her chest.

"Where is she?"

"She wasn't feeling good, and she was refusing to come out of the room." Riley shrugs. "I sent Gibson to check on her, and he ended up taking her to the doctor in town."

I pull my cell from my pocket and check the time. "How long ago was that?"

"About an hour ago."

"And you don't know what was wrong with her?"

"No. I'm sure it's just stress." Riley rests her hand on my bicep. "Don't worry, Greaser. She's fine."

"If she were fine, Gibson would have been able to handle it."

"Not necessarily. Other than the club, Gibson hasn't actually practiced medicine since he was discharged from the military, right?"

"True."

"So maybe he's just being extra cautious because of everything she's been through." She squeezes my arm. "Really, Greaser, she'll be fine. And they'll be home soon."

I hear Riley's words and I want to believe them, but I can't stop the worry that's plaguing me. If Trinity and I wouldn't have gotten into that fight, her stress level wouldn't be so bad it's making her sick. If I had gone after her when she walked out my door, if I would have fought for her, this wouldn't be happening.

If, if, if.

"Why don't you go have a drink with Joker? Kill some time until she gets home?"

"Yeah." I smile at Riley. I really couldn't have asked for a better woman for my best friend. "Thanks, Riles."

"Anytime."

I retrace my steps and head to the bar, where Joker is nursing a beer. Before I can get there, my phone vibrates in my hand, and I lift it to look at the screen.

My stomach drops when I see it's a text from Gibson.

When I click on the notification and read the words, my heart skips a beat and my lungs seize.

We have a problem, G... I can't find her.

CHAPTER TWENTY-NINE

Not everyone is out to get me.

Trinity

Thirty minutes earlier...

"Trinity Milford."

I rise from my seat and make my way toward the nurse who called my name. Gibson follows me, and I twist to press my hand to his chest.

"I'm good," I assure him. "You can wait out here."

"Are you sure? Greaser would want me to stay with you."

"Greaser no longer has a say," I remind him.

I'm nervous enough to be here, and the last thing I need is to have Gibson hovering so he can report back to the man who lost his right to the information the moment he broke his promise.

Gibson doesn't look happy, but he returns to his seat. I follow the nurse through the door and down the hall to an examination room.

"Go ahead and step on the scale so we can get your weight and height."

I do as instructed and am a little surprised to see that I've gained two pounds despite not being able to eat and keep anything down. After recording my height and weight, the nurse takes my temperature and blood pressure. My temp is normal, but my blood pressure is a little high, which isn't surprising considering my nerves.

The nurse opens a drawer and pulls out a gown before handing it to me. "Put this on and the doctor will be in with you shortly."

"Thank you."

When the door closes, I change into the gown. As I'm climbing onto the exam table, there's a knock at the door before it swings open.

"Hello, Ms. Milford." The doctor's smile is friendly and immediately puts me at ease. I was concerned about how I'd react, considering my history with doctors, but so far, so good. "I'm Dr. Chavez." She glances at the file the nurse left on the counter and scans its contents. "What brings you in today?"

"I just haven't been feeling well the last few days. I think it's just stress but my, uh…" Shit. What do I call Gibson? I don't know what I can and can't say. "My family wanted me to be seen by a doctor, just to make sure there's nothing else going on."

"Have you experienced stressful situations recently that make you believe it's only stress causing your symptoms?"

Kidnapped, committed, almost raped, bad breakup… yeah, a few situations.

"Nothing too out of the ordinary," I lie.

"Okay. I see that your blood pressure is a little high." She puts her stethoscope in her ears and presses it to my back.

"Deep breaths for me." She moves to listen to my heart. "Good. Again."

Next she checks my ears, nose, and throat. "Those all look good." She sits on the rolling stool. "You listed vomiting and lack of appetite on the intake form. How long has that been going on?"

"A few days."

"When was your last period?"

I take a deep breath and try to recall when it was, and when I can't, my eyes widen.

"Last period?" she asks again.

I fidget with my hands. "I, um, I don't know."

Dr. Chavez looks at me and smiles. "That's okay. Is there a possibility you could be pregnant?"

"No."

My response is swift, and based on the way her brows shoot up, maybe a little too swift.

"How about we do a pregnancy test?" When I shake my head, she rolls closer to the exam table. "Just to rule it out."

I chew on my lip and nod. "Yeah, okay."

"Good. I'll have my nurse bring you the cup, and she will show you to the bathroom. We'll run the test and have the results in a few minutes. That'll give us a better idea of how to proceed. Okay?"

"Okay."

Dr. Chavez leaves the room, and moments later, a nurse comes in. It's not the same nurse from before and this nurse's attitude sucks.

"Come with me," she says quickly before walking out of the room, leaving me with nothing to do but hop off the table and follow.

She's walking fast, and I pick up my pace to keep up. When she passes the door with the restroom sign next to it, my nerves kick back in. I glance over my shoulder and see that the hallway is empty.

"Ma'am," I call out to her, and she stops to turn and look at me. "The bathroom is right here."

She shakes her head and chuckles. "Oh my gosh, I'm so sorry." She walks toward me. "I'm new and still learning my way around."

I release the breath I didn't even realize I was holding, and relief washes over me. I remind myself that the Lowells are locked up, and even though there are others like them, they don't know where I am. Not everyone is out to get me.

"It's okay."

The nurse walks into the bathroom and sets the cup on the sink. "When you're done, you can slide your sample in there." She points to what looks like a stainless-steel cubby. "I'll be in the room next door to grab it on the other side. You can then return to the exam room and the doctor will be in once she has the results."

"Okay. Thank you."

The nurse leaves me alone, and once I'm done, I slide the sample into the cubby and wash my hands. I turn the light off as I open the door. I return to the exam room and climb onto the table to wait.

Ten minutes pass by and panic sets in. Why is the test taking so long? If it were positive, the doctor would know what's wrong with me and send me on my way, right?

There's a knock on the door before it opens and the nurse who led me to the bathroom enters.

"Congratulations," she says. "You're pregnant."

Shock. That's the only way to describe my reaction to that news. How in the hell did this happen?

You had sex. It's not rocket science Trin.

"I take it that's not what you were expecting?"

The nurse rests her hand on my shoulder. I shake my head, and her fingers curl into my flesh.

"You should be happy," she says and when I look at her, I see that her smile is gone. "Babies are a blessing."

"Of course, it's just…" I shake my head. *Get a grip, Trin. You can freak out later.* "It wasn't planned is all."

"Do you want me to go get the father?"

I narrow my eyes. "What?"

"The father? I assume that's who's out in the waiting room."

"Oh, no, no. He's not the father. I, uh… the father isn't in the picture."

The nurse's eyes narrow. "I see."

"I'm sorry. This isn't your problem. I'll get dressed and get out of your hair."

"Take your time."

The nurse leaves me alone, and I change back into my clothes. Tears burn the back of my eyes, and I don't bother trying to stop them from falling. I swipe at my cheeks before leaning against the door. My breath hitches as I try to suck air into my lungs.

I can't do this. I can't have a baby. I have no clue how to take care of a kid. I don't have a job. Hell, I don't even have my own place to live. Where would I put a crib? Next to the bar in the clubhouse?

Stop! You've known for all of five minutes. You'll figure it all out.

An image of Greaser pops into my mind, and my panic flares. I don't even know if he wants kids. Or if he still wants me. What if he doesn't want any of it? What if the club kicks me out? What if my brother turns on me?

Fear digs its claws into my soul and refuses to let go. So much for figuring it all out.

"Ms. Milford?"

I reach for the tissues on the counter and wipe my face.

"Ms. Milford, is everything okay in there?"

I blow my nose and toss the tissue into the trash. I scrub my eyes, hoping to wipe away the evidence of my tears, and then open the door.

"Are you okay?" the nurse asks.

I nod but fresh tears fill my eyes.

"Would you like to go out the back door?" When I narrow my eyes at her, she shrugs. "The waiting room is full, and I just figured you'd probably like to avoid people. I know I hate when people see me cry." She smiles. "I can let your friend know to meet you in the parking lot," she rushes to add.

I sniffle. "That would be great, thanks."

I follow her down the hall and she opens the door for me. I step outside and turn to thank her, but the words don't make it out of my mouth before her fist connects with my temple. My vision blurs and I sway.

"Babies are a blessing you ungrateful bitch," she sneers.

She hauls her arm back and punches me in the temple again. The last words I hear before my head crashes against the pavement make my blood run cold.

"Greaser isn't going to be happy when he learns your secret."

CHAPTER THIRTY

Of course I came.

Greaser

"*I*'m guessing you're the father."

After receiving Gibson's text, I rallied the brothers and we converged on the doctor's office. When we arrived, the staff still hadn't realized Trinity was gone because Dr. Chavez got sidetracked by an emergency walk-in patient. I demanded to see security footage, as well as any employee files of staff that came into contact with Trinity. Initially, they refused, citing doctor-patient confidentiality, but money talks. Money always talks.

I'd been asked to wait in an exam room while the others waited outside so we don't scare their patients. Joker stayed with me, and then Dr. Chavez just walked in to drop a bombshell.

"Father?"

"Yes." She looks at the document she's holding. "We gave Ms. Milford a pregnancy test and the results are positive."

"Whoa," Joker says. "Congrats bro."

I stand from my chair and pace the tiny room. The walls feel like they're closing in on me, and if it weren't for the fact that I'm still waiting on the info I requested, I'd march out of here and tear up the town on my own to find her.

"I don't…" I inhale deeply and wish I had a joint to take the edge off. "I can't go there right now. When can I see the security footage and employee files?"

"I've got my staff pulling everything together for you," Dr. Chavez assures me. "I really think it would be best to call the police."

"And I really think your office could use the upgrades our *donation* will pay for," I snap. "Maybe add some security guards."

"I understand you're—"

I whirl on Dr. Chavez, but before I can shove her into the wall, Joker wraps an arm around my chest and pulls me back.

I stab a finger in the air at her. "Don't you dare say you fucking understand," I snarl.

"G, you need to calm down," Joker says.

"What I need is Trinity." I shake out of his hold and start pacing again. My heart stutters when I think about her, pregnant with my baby. "I need her and my child. Until I have that, don't tell me to fucking calm down."

A knock on the door pulls me to my feet, and Dr. Chavez opens it. "Here are the files you wanted." The nurse darts a look at me before returning his attention to the doctor. "I checked the security footage, and it looks like Ms. Milford left with Corrine. I've sent a link to your email with the security footage."

"Corinne?" I ask as I snatch the files from the nurse's hands and flip through them to find the right one. When I see the picture inside, I see red.

"Cora," I mumble on an exhale.

How had we not known she was back?

"What?" Joker demands and takes the file from me. "I thought we handled her."

"Who's Cora?" Dr. Chavez asks. I hand her the photo and she narrows her eyes. "No, this is Corrine, like the nurse said. You must be mistaken."

"Her name is Cora," I tell her. "She and I have... *history*."

"She's a relatively new hire, so I don't know much about her personal life."

Dr. Chavez pulls up the security footage she was sent. I watch over her shoulder until I see Trinity being led out the back door by Cora.

"That's odd," Dr. Chavez comments. "I have no idea why she'd be going out the back. We have a strict policy against it."

"There's no telling with Cora."

"I'm so sorry."

"It's not your fault." I pull the documents out of the folder and open the door. "J, let's go. We'll start with Cora's listed address and go from there. Dr. Chavez, can you forward the email with the security footage to me, just in case we need to take a look at it again?"

She frowns. "I really shoul—"

"I'll triple the donation."

She picks up a prescription pad and pen, thrusting both toward me. "Write your email address down."

I provide her with the information, and then Joker and I rush out to the parking lot. Fender spots us and shouts to the others to be quiet so I can fill them in.

"Cora got her," I shout as I jog across the lot to them. "We're going to start with the address in her employee file."

"And Greaser's gonna be a dad!" Joker yells.

"What?" Fender asks.

"Apparently, Trinity is pregnant," I confirm. "That's why she hasn't been feeling well. That's also why it's even more important to get to her."

Fender throws his arm in the air and circles it around. "Let's ride!"

As I throw my leg over my Harley, my phone rings. I pull it from my pocket and see Royal's number flash on the screen. I tap the answer button and put him on speaker.

"Royal, this isn't a good time."

"Royal is indisposed at the moment."

My body stiffens at the voice coming through the line.

"Cora," I breathe. "What the fuck have you done?"

"What I had to," she says nonchalantly.

The others circle around my back as it registers who is on the phone.

"Is Trinity okay?"

"Your skank is fine," Cora snaps.

"I swear to God, if you hurt her, I'll fucking—"

"What? Kill me?" Her laugh fills the air and I cringe. "We both know you won't do that. You've had plenty of reasons to already, and guess what? I'm still breathing."

"If he doesn't, I will." Trainwreck steps closer to me. "Let me talk to my sister."

"Sister?" Cora cackles. "Oh, this just gets better and better."

"What the fuck do you want, Cora?" I snarl.

"You don't know?"

I squeeze my eyes shut and take several deep breaths. "No, I don't know."

"It's simple really," she says. "I want you."

"You can't—"

"Here's how this is going to work," she interrupts. "If

you're not home in twenty minutes, I'll assume you've accepted your bitch's fate."

"You won't get away with this," Fender barks. "Royal isn't the only member on the property."

"I figured as much," Cora says before chuckling. "Really, boys, you don't give me enough credit. Do you seriously think I came alone?"

"What are you talking about?"

"My guys are sweeping the property as we speak."

"You are so fucked," I snarl, knowing all the Soulless Kings will fight to the death. No way Cora's guys live through this.

"Twenty minutes, Greaser."

The call disconnects, and I throw my head back and howl. How the hell had this happened?

"You can break down later," Trainwreck says and slaps me on the back. "Right now, we ride."

"You all heard Cora," Fender says as he walks to his Harley. "We've got twenty minutes to get home. I want to be there in ten."

One Harley after another is fired up, and we do what we do best. We ride... fast and hard. Nine minutes later, we're driving down the road to Soulless Kings' property. When we reach the gate, I don't bother slowing down. I race toward the clubhouse, barely coming to a stop before jumping from my bike and letting it crash to the gravel.

I race up the front steps and through the door, only coming to a stop when I see Cora sitting on the couch. I turn in a circle to take in the armed men around the room. I count twelve. I shift my gaze to Trinity, who's sitting on the floor, her wrists and ankles bound by rope, a gun pointed at her head. Cora jumps up and races toward me.

She launches herself into my arms, and as much as I want

to let her fall to the floor, I don't. Cora is playing a game with me, one where I don't even know the rules.

"I knew you'd come," Cora cries.

Not for you, you crazy bitch.

"Of course I came."

CHAPTER THIRTY-ONE

I love you.

Trinity

"Of course I came."

Greaser's words don't have time to sink in before Cora presses her mouth to his. Bile rises up the back of my throat, and I swallow it down, refusing to get sick in front of her.

Greaser sets Cora on her feet and takes in the men around the room before settling his gaze on me.

"Are you okay?"

"She's fine," Cora snaps. "I'm not a monster."

"You sure about that?"

I flick my gaze beyond Cora and Greaser to see Joker walking through the door, with my brother right behind him, and the others behind him. Tyler focuses on me, and I shake my head slightly, hoping he knows I want him to stay back.

"Fuck you," Cora spits out. "You were always jealous that I wanted Greaser and not your disgusting dick."

"Keep telling yourself that, princess," Joker says.

He's taunting her and I wish he'd stop. I glare at him, but he doesn't even look in my direction.

Greaser glances around the room before returning his attention back to Cora. "Where is everyone, Cora?" he growls.

She laughs and walks toward the couch.

"I have to say, I wasn't expecting you to care about everyone else when I have her." She rolls her eyes as she sits down, her knee brushing my shoulder. "They're fine. Or they will be if you cooperate."

"Where. Are. They?" Greaser asks again.

"Well, they put up a good fight when we stormed the clubhouse, but ultimately," she begins and points to the goons behind her. "My guys were better. They're in the... oh, what is it they called it?" She snaps her fingers. "Oh yes, the Nightmare Room."

"Go get them," Fender orders, and the brothers take a step toward the hall that leads to the basement steps.

Several gunshots ring out and I scream. Then I realize everyone is still standing.

"Next time the bullets will enter flesh and not the ceiling." Cora presses the barrel of her gun to the back of my head. "I told you, I'm not a monster. I don't *want* to kill anyone." She cocks the pistol. "Other than her, of course."

Greaser lunges forward and Cora pulls the trigger. I flinch, expecting excruciating pain, but it doesn't happen. There's a click, followed by an insane laugh.

Cora sobers and warns, "She might not be so lucky next time."

Greaser's eyes flash to mine, and for the first time since I met him, he seems... lost. Broken. A shell of the man I love.

GREASER

Tears roll down my cheeks, and I try to swipe at them with my bound hands. Where did we go wrong? Why did I run the moment things went sideways? Now that I'm faced with the reality of not having a lifetime with him, it's all I want.

"Cora, call your guys off," Greaser demands. "Let's talk about this like adults."

"Do you think I'm that stupid?" she taunts. "The second I call them off, your goons will take me out. No thanks."

"G, what do you want us to do?" Joker asks from across the room. "It's your call."

Greaser locks eyes with me. "Trinity, do you trust me?"

I nod frantically.

He turns in a circle. "Get out of here, all of you."

"Greaser, I don't think—"

"Get out!" Greaser yells, cutting Fender off. "Please. I've got this."

"I'm not leaving her," my brother says.

"Trainwreck, I've got this." Greaser slowly nods. "Trust me."

The brothers hesitate, and I find myself holding my breath. Finally, they all back out through the front door, closing it. I don't know if a plan was made before they arrived, I don't know where they're going, but I know Greaser. And he won't let anything happen to me.

"They're gone, Cora." Greaser walks toward us and nods at the twelve men. "Now, your turn."

The gun appears over my shoulder as she points it at him.

"Ah, ah, ah," Cora tsks. "Did you really think I'd tell them to leave? Seriously, Greaser, you don't give me enough credit." She heaves a sigh. "But I'll throw you a bone. They're under strict instructions not to shoot you unless I give the signal."

Once again, the barrel of the gun is pressed to my temple.

Greaser's eyes widen. "Cora, don't."

"Greaser," I cry. "Please, just... just do whatever she wants."

"You should listen to her," Cora says. "She's quite smart."

"How can I listen to her when I don't even know what the fuck you want?"

"I told you." She scoots over the edge of the couch and sits next to me, shifting the gun to my side. "I want you."

"And you think I'm going to forgive you that easily?"

"I see you still blame me," she says. Cora sniffles and Greaser's face hardens. "How many times do I have to say I'm sorry? It's not my fault our baby died."

"Wait, what?" I say, unable to stop the words.

"He didn't tell you?"

"Uh... no."

"Trinity, don't listen to her," Greaser instructs. "There was nothing to tell."

"Really?" Cora asks. "Well, if you're not going to tell her, I will." Cora shifts so she can look me in the eyes, but she keeps the weapon trained on me. "I got pregnant on accident, but we were over the moon about it." She nods toward my stomach. "Based on your reaction at the doctor, I know you don't think he'd make a good father but, you're wrong. Greaser was amazing through my pregnancy, and he was a great father."

"You're so full of shit!" Greaser shouts.

Cora pulls the trigger, and I shriek, only to hear a click… again. At some point, the click will be replaced by a bullet actually tearing through me.

"Cora, stop," Greaser pleads.

"Fine." She lowers the pistol. "At least while I'm telling the story. Now, where was I?" She waves a hand. "Oh yes, Greaser being so good to me while I was pregnant. He was. And after our son was born, we were going to get married.

But then the baby died. SIDS, the doctors called it. As soon as we buried our son, I left. I was in a very dark place and Greaser only reminded me of the baby."

Cora's story jumbles in my mind. I know she's lying. I know that Greaser would have told me about something like that. He told me he loves me and losing a child isn't something you keep from the person you love. But calling her out isn't going to help me right now. So I play along.

"I'm sorry for your loss," I say, forcing emotion into my words.

"Aw, thank you." Cora swivels her head to look at Greaser. "I can see why you like her. She's sweet."

"She is."

"Anyway, where was I?" Cora scrambles to her feet. "Oh, yes, I left after our son died. But I came back. I got a job, started to rebuild my life." She closes the distance between her and Greaser and wraps her arm around his waist. His muscles tense, but he does his best to hide it. "I kept tabs on you, of course. I knew I'd win you back someday. And imagine my surprise when a woman walks into the doctor's office with none other than a Soulless King. As if that wasn't enough, I overheard them mention your name." Cora drops her arms and turns back around to face me, a grin spreading across her face. "God, I couldn't have asked for a better outcome than her pregnancy test to come back positive. So, I sent a text to my brother." She points over my shoulder to one of the men. "You're not the only one with loyal family ties. My brother came, no questions asked. And he brought reinforcements."

"Great," Greaser barks. "You got Trinity and you got me here. So what's your plan? Kill the woman I love, the woman carrying my child and then what? We can ride off into the sunset?"

Cora shrugs. "Initially, yes, that was the plan."

"Initially?"

Cora walks back toward me. She grips my arm and pulls me to my feet. With my ankles bound together, it's hard to keep my balance, but she keeps me steady.

"Cora, you need to speed things up," one of her men clips out. "Those tranquilizers are going to wear off on the others soon."

"Shut up, Cam," Cora snaps as she glances over her shoulder and then returns her gaze to Greaser. "Forgive my brother. He's impatient."

"I'll forgive him when he stops pointing a damn gun at me," Greaser shouts.

"Fine. Don't forgive him. Doesn't matter to me." Cora wraps her fingers in my hair. "So, do you want to hear my new plan or not?"

Greaser nods but remains quiet. He's fully facing Cora and me, but his eyes continuously dart around the room.

"I'm not going to kill her… today."

Greaser's control snaps. He stalks toward us, but Cora aims the gun at my stomach, forcing him to stop.

"I wouldn't do that," Cora sneers. "I would hate for you to lose two babies."

Cora shifts the gun and points it at Greaser, but he doesn't stop coming. I wait for bullets to start flying but only one person fires their weapon. And when Cora pulls the trigger, there's no click. The bullet hits Greaser, and my heart stops.

Greaser drops his gaze to his arm and narrows his eyes when he sees blood trickle out of the bullet hole to drip onto the floor.

"You shot me," he mumbles before lifting his head and glaring at her. "You fucking shot me."

"I did," Cora agrees. "And now they will too."

When he takes another step forward, chaos ensues. Soulless King after Soulless King storm the clubhouse, and bullet after bullet whizzes through the air as they exchange gunfire with Cora's men. I throw myself to the floor and try to crawl away, but my movement is hampered when a heavy weight settles on top of me.

"I've got you, sweetheart."

I turn my head and lock eyes with Greaser. He smiles, but it quickly turns to a grimace when he tries to wrap his arm around my waist to drag me to safety.

"Motherfucker," he groans through clenched teeth.

"What were you thinking?" I whisper harshly. "She had a gun pointed at you. And there were twelve more behind her."

"You really want to get into this now?"

A bullet strikes the floor a few feet from my head, and I jump.

No. No I don't.

Greaser presses a quick kiss to my lips before reaching his arm down to grab his own knife from his boot. He slices through the ropes binding my wrists and ankles. Then he shoves away from me to stand and whirls toward the action.

I roll to my side and see bodies littering the floor. Dead bodies. And not one of them is a Soulless King. I watch as Greaser takes a stance next to Tyler and the others, all of them with their guns pointed toward the bar. I look in that direction and see Cora's reflection in the mirror behind the liquor. She's crouched down and using the bar as a shield.

What the hell? How is she still alive?

I bang a fist into the floor to get Greaser's attention, and when he glances at me, I mouth the word 'weapon' to him. He gives a faint shake of his head, but I don't let up. Finally, he taps my brother on the shoulder. I see their lips moving, but I can't hear what they're saying. After what appears to be a disagreement, Tyler bends to pull a gun out of his boot and slides it across the floor to me.

I lift it in my hands and test the weight of it, the feel of it. I don't like it. Not one bit, but that doesn't matter. One way or another, Cora has to be dealt with.

We all tried to play by her rules, but I'm done playing.

I crawl across the room, dodging bodies and pools of blood, until I reach the barstools. I look back toward Greaser, and the determination etched into his expression fortifies me. He, along with the others, nods. They have my back.

I scramble to my feet and turn my body toward the bar, giving the Soulless Kings my back.

"Stand the fuck up," I demand of Cora. When she doesn't, I add, "Don't be a coward."

I watch in the mirror as she slowly stands, and I aim my brother's gun at her. My hands are steady, but on the inside, I'm a quaking mess.

"You won't kill me," Cora taunts. "You know it would hurt Greaser."

"Wouldn't count on that," Greaser shouts across the room.

I shrug. "He's right. I'm not too concerned about how it would make him feel."

"Pull the trigger, Trin," my brother yells. "What are you waiting for?"

That's a good question.

Cora laughs hysterically. "I knew it. You wo—"

I squeeze the trigger, and Cora drops to the floor. My arms go limp, and I crumble against the bar. Greaser rushes forward and drops to my side.

"Jesus," he whispers and cups my cheeks. "That was... fucking hot."

I crack a smile, but it doesn't reach my eyes. I've now killed two people, and as much as it was justified, I know I have to figure out how to be okay with it.

"Damn, Trinity," Tyler says when he steps up next to us. "That was a nice shot."

"Thanks," I mumble.

Greaser helps me to my feet and wraps his arms around me. "I am so sorry this happened."

"It's not your fault," I assure him, pressing my cheek to his chest and focusing on his heartbeat.

"G, you need to let Gibson take a look at your arm."

I lift my head and look at Fender before dropping my gaze to where Cora shot Greaser. I press my hand over the wound. "He's right."

"He can look at it later. Right now, I just want to be with you."

My heart melts. He wants what I want.

I think.

I grab his hand and flatten it on my stomach. "You mean us?"

Greaser's eyes become suspiciously shiny, and he grins. "Yeah. I want you both."

I throw my arms around his neck, and he lifts me up so I can wrap my legs around him.

"I love you."

EPILOGUE

I have many brothers, many men who I would die for, kill for, who I live for. And now I have another one... perhaps the most important one.

Greaser

Three months later...

"Is everything still set for tonight?"

I squeeze Trinity's hand and lean over to press my lips to hers. She's the only woman I know who can worry about her brother when she's about to find out the sex of her baby. I break the kiss and grin at her.

"Sweetheart, it's all taken care of."

"Okay, good." She adjusts on the exam table, and the paper drape shifts to expose her growing belly. "I would hate for anything to go wrong. Tyler deserves this."

"He does. And nothing is going to go wrong," I assure her.

Trinity nods but then her eyes widen, and she slaps her free hand on her forehead. "Oh my god, I forgot to order the cake."

I chuckle at her. She's right, she did forget, but I didn't. Before I can reassure her, there's a knock on the door, and the doctor steps in.

"How are we doing today?" the doctor asks.

Trinity heaves a sigh before forcing a smile. "We're doing good."

The doctor squeezes some jelly onto Trinity's stomach and then slides the ultrasound wand back and forth until a picture forms on the screen.

"So, are you wanting to know the sex today?"

"Yes," we both say in unison.

The doctor chuckles, and a thumping sound begins. "There's the heartbeat." She shifts the wand. "And everything looks good. He's the perfect size for sixteen weeks."

"He?"

"Yes, he. Congratulations, you're having a boy."

The doctor prints out several ultrasound pictures and hands them to me. She leaves the room, and Trinity's eyes fill with tears.

I grab a few tissues and wipe the jelly from her stomach. After helping her up, she throws her arms around me.

"We're having a son." She looks up at me. "A little boy, like you."

"We are."

I rub circles over her back. How the hell did I get so lucky?

After Cora's body was disposed of, Trinity and I had a long talk about everything Cora said. I explained how Cora and I had sex a few times and assured her that it didn't mean anything. I told her how Cora showed up with a newborn and a birth certificate, claiming me as the father, but that she was lying.

Trinity was livid upon hearing the truth, but not at me. All of her rage was aimed at Cora and the universe. So many things had to happen in order for a perfect storm to be created. A perfect storm named Cora. What were the odds that Cora would be a nurse at the very doctor's office where Trinity learned about her pregnancy?

Like I said... perfect storm.

"We should probably head home," Trinity says, pulling me from my thoughts.

I glance at the clock and nod. "Yeah, we should. We've got the vote in an hour and the party tonight."

"Are we going to tell everyone the sex? Or do you want to wait?"

"I don't know. What do you think?"

Trinity shrugs. "I don't want to take away from Tyler. Today is about him."

"True," I agree. "But I think he'll be thrilled to learn he's going to have a nephew."

"He will be, but…"

"Why don't we leave it up to him? Once the vote is over, we'll tell him and if he wants us to wait to tell the others, we will."

Trinity nods. "That'll work."

We take our time getting home, both of us wanting to revel in our news a little while longer. When I finally pull up to the clubhouse, Trainwreck steps out onto the porch to greet us.

"What took you so long?" he asks as he jogs down the steps.

"Hi to you too," Trinity laughs and gives him a hug.

"Yeah, yeah, hi." He laughs and rocks back on his heels. "So, am I having a niece or nephew?"

Before either of us can respond, Fender comes outside to join us.

"Finally," he says. "I'd like to get church started."

"Prez, we still have a few minutes," Trainwreck grumbles.

"You have all the time in the world," Fender says. "Greaser doesn't."

Trainwreck doesn't know we're voting on his patch today. He thinks it's a normal meeting. He'll be invited in after we vote, but until then, he needs to stay in the dark.

"Sweetheart, if you want to tell him while I'm in church, I'm fine with that."

"Are you sure?" she asks.

"He's sure," Trainwreck snaps and then rolls his eyes. "Sorry. But the suspense is killing me."

"Trinity, put him out of his misery before I do," Fender instructs, laughing. "Greaser, let's go."

I follow my president into the clubhouse, and we make our way to the meeting room. All patched members are already present, and after depositing our weapons into the designated box, Fender and I take our seats.

Piston bangs the gavel. "Let's get this meeting started."

"I know we have a lot of business to discuss with the upcoming criminal trial for the Lowells. We also have to give updates on our search for the trafficking ring teams. But that's not why we're here today." Fender looks around the room. "Being a member of the Soulless Kings is a privilege, one we all take seriously. We have our policies and procedures in place in order to honor the sanctity of the club. And with that in mind, we have an important vote today, the most important vote: whether or not to give a prospect a patch."

Fender turns to me and nods. "Go ahead, G."

I stand up to give my nomination. "I nominate Trainwreck, aka Tyler Milford, to become a permanent patched member of the Soulless Kings MC."

I look to Riker on my right.

"Trainwreck is loyal," he says before looking to Curly on his right.

"Trainwreck is dedicated," Curly says and then looks to Gibson.

"Trainwreck is honorable."

Gibson looks to his right. Each patched member lists a quality Trainwreck possesses that makes him the perfect candidate. When we reach the end of the line, Fender lifts the patch in question.

"All in favor of Trainwreck receiving his patch, thump twice."

And just like that, the Soulless Kings grow by one member.

"Riker, will you go get Trainwreck and bring him in, please?" Fender asks.

While we wait for the two of them to return, we remain silent and force ourselves to appear upset. Voting in a new member is exciting, but policy states we don't celebrate until the patch is accepted. And we are in no way permitted to appear happy.

Trainwreck precedes Riker into the room, and he's grinning wildly. When he sees all of our faces, he stops short and scowls.

"What's wrong?" He shifts his gaze to me. "Did something happen with the traffickers?

"Trainwreck, sit down," Fender barks.

He shuffles to the only empty seat in the room and sits. His shoulders are tense, his face red with frustration.

"Spit it out," he snaps.

"We have a problem," Fender begins. "You're a prospect, and as such, there are certain things you shouldn't be involved in."

"Seriously?" Trainwreck shoots to his feet. "I do everything you ask. I never question—"

"That is why we'd like to give you this." Fender lifts the new patch.

"What?"

"We voted and we'd like you to become a patched member of the Soulless Kings."

"But..." Trainwreck drops back into the chair. "I thought... You're serious."

"Very serious," I tell him. "Once you put this patch on, there's no taking it off. This isn't a marriage where you can file paperwork and get a divorce if you change your mind. Once a Soulless King, always a Soulless King."

"Wow." Trainwreck gets to his feet and walks toward Fender. "Thank you. I won't let you down, Prez."

Fender hands him the patch, and cheers erupt around the room. Piston bangs the gavel to quiet everyone down.

"I know you won't let us down," Fender states. "If we thought you would, this would be a very different meeting. Now, there's a party tonight to celebrate."

"Right." Trainwreck backs toward the door. "I'll go start getting things set up."

"Trainwreck." He stops and looks at me. "You're not a prospect anymore. You don't do grunt work. Get Royal to do it."

"I, um..."

"What is it?" Fender asks. "Your voice matters now, so spit it out."

"It's just... Royal probably isn't the best choice for grunt work right now."

"Why not?"

"He's still beating himself up about what happened, about Cora and her men taking him by surprise and gaining access to the clubhouse. I'm pretty sure he's high out of his mind and in no condition to do anything."

"Jesus," Riker mutters. "I'll go handle him."

Riker disappears from the room, and Fender nods at Piston to bang the gavel and end the meeting.

"Meeting adjourned."

Most of the members leave the room. Fender and Joker go to help Riker. Trainwreck sticks behind until we're the only two left. The grin he was sporting when he entered the room is back in place, and I shake my head.

"She told you, didn't she?"

"She did."

"Why didn't you share the news with the others?" I ask, confused because he's clearly proud of the fact that he's going to have a nephew.

Trainwreck shrugs. "Not my news to share, brother."

Brother.

I have many brothers, many men who I would die for, kill for, who I live for. And now I have another one… perhaps the most important one.

"That sounds pretty good," I say.

"What does?"

"Brother. What would you say if I made that more legal?"

"Are you asking if you can marry my sister?"

"And if I am?"

"I'd laugh in your face and remind you that what she does with her life is up to her, not me. Remember, she's free. She can do anything she wants."

Does he know something I don't?

"Right."

I brush past him, but his voice stops me at the door.

"You know she'll choose you, every single time."

I glance over my shoulder at him, and he shrugs.

"She's free and she still chooses you. So yeah, make the brother thing legal."

Six months later, after the birth of our son, Trenton Tyler, Trinity and I do just that.

NEXT IN THE SOULLESS KINGS MC SERIES

Riker...

I'm the Enforcer of the Soulless Kings for a reason. I do what I'm told, no matter how grizzly, how dangerous, how inhumane. And I live for it. I like hurting people, teaching them a lesson they couldn't possibly forget. But even I have my limits. I don't hurt women, children, or animals.

In fact, if I catch you crossing that line, I'll make you pay... with your life. So when another local MC reaches out to us for help with a *traffic* problem, I jump on it. The problem is, I don't realize exactly who I'll be working with until I come face to face with her. Yeah, that's right, *her*. It doesn't take me long to realize why they call her Looney Tunes, and I kinda love the fact that there's a female version of me out there. And I'm willing to burn down her walls to prove we're two sides to the same coin.

Luna...

Looney Tunes. That's what they call me. And I've earned the nickname. I embrace it, embody it, revel in it. Some would say I have a screw loose, but I don't care. I'm the President of the Devil's Handmaidens MC: Oregon Chapter and my ability to handle the more unsavory side of life makes me good at what I do.

So when I have to enlist the help of another MC, I don't like it. Not even when their Enforcer stirs up fantasies I've worked hard to ignore. I don't do relationships, or even one night stands. They're too much trouble, too distracting. And it's never been a problem for me… until him. Can I let him in enough to get the job done without compromising a life system that works for me? I don't know, but I'm sure as hell going to try.

ABOUT THE AUTHOR

Andi Rhodes is an author whose passion is creating romance from chaos in all her books! She writes MC (motorcycle club) romance with a generous helping of suspense and doesn't shy away from the more difficult topics. Her books can be triggering for some so consider yourself warned. Andi also ensures each book ends with the couple getting their HEA! Most importantly, Andi is living her real life HEA with her husband and their boxers.

For access to release info, updates, and exclusive content, be sure to sign up for Andi's newsletter at andirhodes.com.

ALSO BY ANDI RHODES

Broken Rebel Brotherhood

Broken Souls

Broken Innocence

Broken Boundaries

Broken Rebel Brotherhood: Complete Series Box set

Broken Rebel Brotherhood: Next Generation

Broken Hearts

Broken Wings

Broken Mind

Bastards and Badges

Stark Revenge

Slade's Fall

Jett's Guard

Soulless Kings MC

Fender

Joker

Piston

Greaser

Riker

Trainwreck

Squirrel

Gibson

Satan's Legacy MC

Snow's Angel

Toga's Demons

Magic's Torment

Printed in Great Britain
by Amazon

43865651R00131